After Dark

By Manly Wade Wellman

AFTER DARK
THE OLD GODS WAKEN

After Dark

MANLY WADE WELLMAN

DOUBLEDAY & COMPANY, INC.

GARDEN CITY, NEW YORK

All of the characters in this book are fictitious, and any resemblance to actual persons, living or dead, is purely coincidental.

for
my Southern mountains
and the seers, poets, and friends I have found among them

When you have a memory out of darkness, tell to a seer, to a poet, and to a friend, that which you remember: And if the seer say, I see it—and if the poet say, I hear it—and if the friend say, I believe it: Then know of a surety that your remembrance is a true remembrance.

Leabhran Mhor Gheasadiareachd (*The Little Book of the Great Enchantment*)

Let no one scorn the friendly tale,
Or doubt, unkind, its shadowed truth. . . .
—Frank Shay, *Here's Audacity*

After Dark

I

You can feel right small and alone amongst those foresty mountains, even by the light of the day; and the sun was a-sagging down toward a toothy sawback of heights there at the west. I slogged my way along the track I'd been told was a shortcut to where the singing would be. I traveled light, as usual. I toted a blanket with an extra shirt and socks rolled into it, a soogin sack with a couple of tins of rations and a poke of cornmeal, and of course my silver-strung guitar. My wide black hat had summer sweat inside the band. And I was glad for roominess inside my old boots, resoled I can't recollect how many times.

That track was a sort of narrow, rutted road. It must have been run there when wolves and buffaloes walked it, and Indians hunted after them before the first white man was even dreamt of in those parts. Off to right and left, pointy peaks and ridges shagged over with trees. They looked to hold memories of witchmen and bottomless pools; of Old Devlins, who watches by a certain lonesome river ford, though folks declare he died long years back; such things, and the Behinder that nobody's air seen yet and lived to tell of, because it jumps you down from behind; and a lot more, scary to think about.

Now, a cleared-off space to the left there. I minded myself of how I'd heard once what had fallen out there a hundred years or so back. How Confederate soldiers had scooped up a bunch they allowed were Union bush-whackers—maybe rightly called that, maybe not. An un-lucky thirteen of those, a couple of them just boys a-start-ing their teens. They'd sat the thirteen down, side by side on a long log, and then tore down with their guns and killed them. Afterward, they dug a ditch right there and buried them. No log there now, naturally, after all that long time. But folks vow up and down that after dark the log comes back again to where once it lay. And that those unlucky thirteen dead ones come out of their ditch and sit down on it, maybe speak to you if you walk past in the night.

It wasn't full night yet, as I've said; but I thought to my-self, something sort of snaky showed there, like the shadow of the log. And I made my long legs stretch themselves longer to get away from the place, quick as I could.

Whatever was I there to do? Well, gentlemen, I'd been a-going through the county seat, and there were signs nailed up to tell folks about a big sing of country music, along about sundown, the sort of thing I've always loved. It would be into the hills near to where a settlement name of Immer had once lived and died. I'd seen more signs about it, in Asheville and over the mountains in Gatlinburg and so on. Since that was my kind of music, I'd reckoned I'd just go and hark at it and maybe even join in with it.

"Along about sundown"—that was all the posters had said about the time, and it would be along about sundown right soon now. But when I rounded a bend of the track past a bluff, I could see where I'd been headed. There was a hollow amongst the heights, with a paved road looped into it from the far side. There stood a ruined old building of different kinds of mountain stone, big as a courthouse, with torn-down walls round about it. That had been an old, old hospital folks told about; built for Immer and the other houses in the neighborhood by a doctor—Dr. Sam Ollebeare he'd been named—who wanted to give care to the people in those wild places. When he'd died after long years of his good work, the hospital had gone to ruin, for no other doctor had taken over. Ruin had likewise come, they said, to the houses where folks had lived in Immer and round there. The folks had gone off some place else or maybe just died or just uglied away.

Rows of cars were parked in a big level space, and people milled round. I saw that amongst the ruined walls was a big hole they used for an entrance. The folks out of the cars walked thataway and paid their money to a man who waited for it to be paid. A vine grew up the tumbledown wall, with white evening flowers on it. To me, it seemed like as if the flowers watched while the man took in the money. I waited for the way to clear out before I walked up to him.

"Admission two dollars," he said, in a sort of fadeaway voice.

I took me a long look at him. He wasn't big, wouldn't have come air much higher than my shoulder. He had a sort of tea-colored face, with a right big mane of hair darker than mine, combed back from it. His black coat came to his knees, like a preacher's, but it was buttoned right up to the neck. His black pants fitted him snug and his black shoes looked to be home-cobbled. Something about the coat and pants looked like homemade stuff too. There were big saddle stitches at all the seams.

"Two dollars," he said again, like a judge in court a-telling you a fine.

"Hark at me, sir," I said, and smiled. "My name's John.

I pick on this guitar, and I sort of reckoned I might could pick on it here tonight, a little bit."

He looked me up and down, with midnight eyes that didn't seem like regular eyes. Maybe he didn't much value the way I was dressed, with my old jeans pants and a faded hickory shirt and that wide old country hat.

"John," he repeated me my name. "I don't believe that you've been sent for to sing here, John."

Just inside that broken-down gateway hole, I saw a couple more men, a-waiting and a-watching me. They were dressed like the gatekeeper, long black coats, with swept-back hair. They might could have been brothers to him, all brothers in a not very friendly family.

"Hold on," said another voice, soft but plain.

Somebody came at us. He was middling tall, dark-haired like those others, but his hair was cut and combed like as if it had been styled for him. He wore good store clothes, a black and white check jacket that fitted him like a special-made sheath for a knife, and his gray pants belled out stylish at the bottoms. On his sharp-nosed face he had smoked glasses, though the sun was as good as down over the heights at the west.

"Hold on," he said again as he came near. "What does this man want?"

"He says he wants to sing," mumbled the money-taking one, and he didn't sound in favor of my a-doing that.

The stylish fellow set his glasses on me. "Can you play that guitar with those pretty, shiny strings?" he inquired me.

"There's been those who've been nice enough to say I could."

"The old, old songs?" was his next question. "Traditional?"

"Them, and now and then I make me one."

"Very well," and he grinned white teeth at me. "Make one for us to decide on. About who you are and what you do."

Another bunch of folks was there to go in at the gate. They stood and watched while I tuned my guitar here and there, and thought quick of some sort of tune for what I'd been bid to make up out of my head. I tried some chords; something a-sounding like maybe "Rebel Soldier," though not much:

> "You ask me what my name is,
> And what I'm a-doing here—
> They call me John the Wanderer
> Or John the Balladeer.
>
> "I've sung at shows and parties,
> I've sung at them near and far,
> All up and down and to and fro,
> With my silver-strung guitar."

The listening folks clapped me for that much, but the one with the glasses just cocked his head, didn't nod it. "Go on," he said, and I went on:

> "Sometimes I travel on buses,
> Sometimes I travel on planes,
> Sometimes I travel a-walking
> On the country roads and lanes.
>
> "In the homes of the rich and mighty
> Sometimes I've laid me down,
> Sometimes on the side of a mountain
> On the cold and lonesome ground."

By then, they all were a-listening so you could purely feel it. I stuck together a last verse:

> "I've made up my songs and ballads
> And sung them both far and near,
> But the best of them all I've whispered
> With only myself to hear."

More handclapping when I finished. The man with the glasses smiled again.

"Not bad, John," he said. "Not bad at all. Very well, come in and sing that one for us tonight. You seem to have a ready gift."

He sort of stabbed his smooth-gloved hand at me, and I took it. It was nowhere the size of my big one, but it was strong when he gripped for just a second and then let go. "Come along," he said, and led me inside. I made out that his boot heels were built up to make him look taller.

They'd set up all right for their singing. The ruins of the old stone hospital and its outside wall closed a big space in. Logs had been strung in rows, and folks sat on them, maybe the way those bushwhackers had sat to be shot down. They all faced toward a stage made of poles and split puncheons, with canvas hiked up at the back.

"My name's Brooke Altic," said the man, with his white-toothed smile. "I'm running this program. We'll play it by ear, more or less—impromptu. Out behind there are the other performers. Go and get acquainted, John. I'll call you to sing your songs when it seems to be the right time."

He walked away, on his built-up boots.

I went behind the stage. Some lanterns hung from the trees there, and musicians sort of milled round. I saw instrument cases scattered here and yonder, like shoes flung off by giants. To one side, four fellows in black shirts and pants were softly playing together—guitar, banjo, fiddle, and bass. Nearer in, I saw a man I knew—turkey-faced Jed Seagram with his big rodeo hat and green rodeo shirt and the banjo he knew maybe about three honest breaks on. He was a-talking to a girl in dark red slacks, with a fine tumble of bright yellow hair and a guitar.

"All I was a-saying, Miss Callie, is that you hold that guitar funny," Jed was a-lecturing at her.

"Well then, listen to what I say," she told him back. "This happens to be my guitar, and I'll happen to hold it whichever way I choose."

Fire in her words, I tell you. Jed squinched his turkey face and walked off away from her. I walked toward her.

"The way you got Jed told was the right way," I felt like a-saying to her. "Wherever he is, Jed always wants to run things."

She looked at me with a sweet, round face, big blue eyes in it, and a mouth as red as a cherry. "Oh," she said, and smiled. "I know who you are; I've heard you with your guitar at Flornoy College. You're John."

"Yes, ma'am."

Somebody else was there, a-scowling. "Are you having trouble, Callie?"

"I was, but I took care of it," she replied him. "John, this is a friend of mine, Mr. Jackson Warren."

He was a man my age or nearly, maybe five feet ten, with two-three silver streaks in his black hair. His tan jacket and pants weren't as fancy as Brooke Altic's, but they looked good on his square shoulders and straight legs. We shook hands together.

"Did she call you John?" he asked. "Then I've heard of you, I think."

"I'm right proud for so many folks to know me by name."

"And," he said, "you seem to have met Miss Callie Gray here. I'm visiting her father, Mr. Ben Gray. He lives over toward where Immer used to be."

"And there's no chance now of my hoping for the guitar-picking prize, now that John's here," said Callie, though she didn't make herself mourn over it.

It was the first I'd heard about prizes. "There's no such a thing as no chance, ma'am," I said, and she smiled at me. I saw Jackson Warren smile, too. He kept his eyes on Callie.

A loudspeaker made itself heard. "Good evening, ladies and gentlemen," said Brooke Altic's voice over it. "Welcome to our little festival of folk music. You were kind to join us. Let's start by listening to the band that calls itself the Four Seekers."

That dark-dressed bunch carried its instruments up the steps at a trot. Lanterns hung overhead to light them up there. I thought they looked like the men in the black coats who had met me at the gateway. They bunched together and went right into a song, pretty handy at it, all their strings at once. It was the kind of tune you'd call lonesome, with a wail to it and a long moan in the harmony underneath. They sang with it, but the words were hard to understand. "Way, way," it sounded like as if they sang. "Way, way—" What kind of words were those, if they were words?

But from where I stood a little clear off from the steps, I could see the audience a-sitting up with tight faces to hark at it, the way you'd think that was its main business in life. When the Four Seekers finished, the whole crowd clapped and clapped. The Four Seekers picked and sang again, another sneaky, minory thing. When they finished and bowed, they got a right much handclapping again.

Brooke Altic came back center stage, mike in hand, to introduce a father and son named Hunter. They played

fiddles, duets of "Fire in the Mountains" and "Laurel Lonesome" and "The Devil's Dream." Sometimes they played
just a rolling harmony, sometimes one would take the tune
and the other would pick his strings like a banjo. They
were good, and the audience let them know it.

After them: "Miss Callie Gray and her guitar," announced Altic.

She got up there, little and pretty and a-smiling. She
picked in what sounded like a modal scale, minor-sounding
and yet not minor. Sweetly she sang:

> "Come over the bourn, Bessy,
> Come over the bourn, Bessy,
> Sweet Bessy, come over to me;
> And I shall thee take
> And my dear lady make,
> Before all other that ever I did see. . . ."

On she went, with a verse to answer that, and it turned
out it was meant to be the old-timey English people
a-talking to Queen Elizabeth, the great Queen Elizabeth
back then. I harked, and wondered myself at how good a
song it was. When she was done and made a curtsey at the
end, she got her round of applause.

"That was beautiful," said Jackson Warren beside me,
and it was.

Other performers followed; it's hard to recollect all of
them. I liked one set of clog dancers in special.

Finally Brooke Altic announced: "Now for a stranger in
our midst, who says his name's John. I want him to play
the song he made up about himself."

I went up there with my guitar. Right off, folks began to
holler things:

"I vow, that's no stranger whatever!"

"That's John—how you come on, John?"

And yells and handclappings before I even started in. It was good to know I had friends or, anyway, well-wishers out there.

As I'd been bid, I sang the song Altic had mentioned, and they purely tore up the logs with their hollering and whooping. Altic came close to me with his grin. "Listen, John," he said, "might you know a scary song—a ghost song? I particularly like that sort."

"I'll try one," I said to him, and when the racket died down he stuck the mike in my face.

"Friends," I said, "let me try a song they call 'Murder Bull.' I learnt it from a Texas man, who said the thing truly happened in his part of the world."

I struck a chord, then another chord, to make sure I was sure of the tune, and started out:

> "When the night is dark and stormy
> And the ghost wind moans and chills,
> They tell about the Murder Bull
> That roams the Texas hills.
>
> "It was at that big roundup
> In eighteen eighty-four,
> Two riders claimed a stray bull calf
> On the old Red River shore.
>
> "He wasn't much to fight for,
> But Jillson's hate was black;
> He fired a shot through Graham's chest
> And it came out the back.
>
> "Graham drew his bowie knife
> And struck in Jillson's side,
> And both fell down, and no one knew
> Which was the first that died."

"Ohh," I heard a pretty-dressed lady say from the front log as I went on:

> "The others at the roundup,
> They gathered round and said,
> "There's none of us will claim that calf,
> Now both of them are dead."

> "A running iron they heated,
> The calf they roped and tied,
> And in big, burning letters
> Spelled MURDER on his hide."

I heard the whole listening bunch draw in their breath.

> "They drove him out to roam the hills,
> And when his time was full,
> He grew up big and terrible,
> The maverick Murder Bull.

> "And many a year's been born and died,
> But still he prowls at night
> With MURDER branded on his flank
> In letters red and bright.

> "If you live in East Texas,
> Be always on your guard,
> Because some night the bull may come,
> Walk right into your yard.

> "While you sit in there, watching
> The fire that dulls and dies,
> He'll come up to your window
> With MURDER in his eyes.

> "Then turn and look the other way
> And hold your frightened breath,

For if you face the Murder Bull
His eyes will give you death."

I finished and laid my palm on the guitar strings to make them quiet. Then I bowed and waited.

There was dead silence all over, for while I counted about half a dozen ticks. Then they broke out with their racket. I walked off, and Brooke Altic met me as I came down the steps from the stage. He grabbed my hand in his thin, strong one and shook it.

"That was magnificent, John," he said. "Listen to them applaud."

We waited until the noise died down. Then Brooke Altic walked up there again and took the mike in hand. Callie Gray and Jackson Warren came up on my right and left.

"That song's a great one," said Callie. "It made me shiver but it's great."

"You're a true artist, John," said Warren.

"I wonder myself why he asked me to sing a ghost song," I told them.

Meanwhile, Altic's voice was a-coming on loud over the public address system. "Ladies and gentlemen," he said, "thank you for seeming to enjoy our efforts here tonight. Now it's time to give the prizes."

One of the black-coated men, likely the one who'd taken up the money at the gate, brought a tray with gold-shining cups.

"I'm going to read out the names in the various categories," announced Altic. "Please clap for whoever you think should win."

He read out the names for fiddle, banjo, guitar, dance, and so on. There was clapping for name after name, but most of all came when, in the guitar class, Altic said, "John."

"Go on up," said Warren, and I went up. Several other winners were there, the fiddling Hunters amongst them. Altic gave out the cups, one by one. Mine was a beauty, a round one to hold better than half a pint, with a foot to stand on. We all of us bowed our thanks and left the stage. Warren looked at the cup.

"This may well be worth a fortune," he said.

"And now, my friends," Altic boomed over the system, "you may have heard that this event has been staged to raise money for a good cause, the advancement of freedom and justice and progress. It is possible that some of you would care to help that cause further along. I'm going to ask the Four Seekers to play for us while we pass the hat."

The Four Seekers hurried on stage and went into another wild, drum-rolly piece of music that seemed to flicker round them in the lantern light. While they did that, I saw the black-coated fellows out in the aisles with little baskets, a-passing them back and forth like for a collection in church. People along the rows put things in the baskets and handed them back. One of the fellows walked to where we three stood beside the steps to the stage and held out his basket.

"Thank you, but I don't reckon I will," I said, a-looking into his basket. It was three quarters full of money bills and what looked like jewels—ladies' rings and bracelets and so on. That was a rich harvest without anything from me, and no I reckon about it. He looked at me, with deep eyes and a nose pooched out like the beak of a bird. Then he went on past me.

"So you didn't contribute, John," said Jackson Warren, close to my ear.

"No. I didn't feel like it."

"Neither did I." He barely whispered that. "Maybe you suspect this crowd."

"Maybe."

"Well," he said, "they're Shonokins."

"Shonokins?" I didn't recollect air a-hearing that name before. "What's that mean?"

"Keep your voice down." His eyes watched mine. "Since you're here, it's high time you found out. You and I would do well to work together, perhaps. Where are you staying tonight?"

"Why," I said, "I hadn't much thought about that. Likely I'll find a place to make a fire and roll up in my blanket."

Callie came up beside Warren. "Come with us, John," she invited me. "My father knows who you are. He'll be glad to have you at our house."

"And you and I can talk," Warren added on, and it sounded to me like as if I'd be a-hearing something right strange, maybe right unchancy.

II

Jackson Warren's car was old and dim and rusty, with two-three dents that told you it had been bumped in its time; but when he got it out of the parking area with Callie a-sitting at his side and me with my gear in the back seat, it ran all right, strong and smooth. It had to, on the bumpy, wiggly dirt road we followed, with the rows of big, dark trees to either side.

"This is more or less my father's road nowadays," said Callie. "Nobody much lives along this stretch. It hooks on to another track outside our place, the old Immer Road."

"Immer," I repeated her. "That's what the old settlement was called."

"In German, that means something like always or forever," said Warren.

"Likely it was just somebody's name once," said Callie. "But, John, we wondered why you didn't contribute there at the singing."

"Something told me not to," I said.

"And something told you right," said Warren. "Apparently you have a good sense of what to do and what not to do."

"You were a-going to tell me about the Shonokins," I reminded him.

And, as he drove, he told me about the Shonokins.

Not many folks knew any more about them than I'd known when he'd first said the name to me. They were an old, old people, he allowed, who'd been a-making themselves hard to find or even to notice over nobody could say how many years. Warren knew about them because he'd worked up North with somebody named John Thunstone—"The same good name you have, John"—and Thunstone had managed to do things against them, even in New York City. But lately, they'd started to show up here, in these mountains.

It wasn't easy, Warren went on to tell, to make out a Shonokin as different from ordinary folks. One way was by their eyes, which in the daytime had a pupil that ran up and down like a cat's instead of a round circle. And on their hands, the third fingers were longer than the middle fingers.

"Always you see males," said Warren, "if you see any Shonokins at all. I've heard Thunstone say that he wonders if there are any female Shonokins."

I thought that over to myself for a second or two. "If they don't have females, how does science explain where Shonokins come from?" I asked finally.

"Science doesn't recognize that there are any such things as Shonokins."

He'd told all that in a few words, and he brightened up when Callie allowed that he talked like a scientist himself.

"No, Callie," he said, a-rolling her name on his tongue. "I'm just an obscure seeker for the truth, old enough to be your father."

"You're no such thing." She smiled back. "My father's Ben Gray, and he's near about old enough to be your father."

"You're very kind," he sort of chuckled, "but my hair's popping out in pale patches while I study the way the Shonokins are coming out of their hiding in these parts. I wonder if John believes any of this?"

"Why shouldn't I believe it?" I came back at him from where I sat behind. "You sound honest enough to tell it."

About then he brought us into a hollow, with wooded hills just barely to be seen all round about. There, among some pines, stood a cabin. It was made of logs and easy to see just then, because the chinking had been picked out to let in summer air and light, and now it let out light at us from inside. It shone sort of like a jack-o'-lantern, rosy streaks betwixt the dark logs. As Warren stopped the car in the yard, the front door opened and a man stepped out on the puncheon porch.

"Oh," he said, "it's youins, back from that singing. Come on in the house."

He blinked down at me from the porch. We got out and walked toward the cabin. "John," said Callie, "this is my daddy, Mr. Ben Gray."

He was a ready-looking, middling built man in work pants and shirt, with lots of curly hair as gray as his name. He had a good face, shaped like a wedge, and there was a plenty of room at the top of it for sense. His eyes were deep-set and his nose was long and straight, with under it a moustache like a frosty strip of fur. "John," he said at me. "John."

"Yes, sir," I said. "I'm John."

He studied the guitar under my arm. "I reckon you must be the John that just goes by that name. The one we hear tell all sorts of good things about. Then you're kindly welcome to my house and aught I can do to make you comfortable."

"I do thank you, sir," I said.

"Don't call me sir; I wasn't nair an officer in the war. Just a sergeant. Come round, John, come on in."

We went up the porch steps and followed him inside. I already felt a right much at home.

There was a great big front room, the whole width of the house, and doors to more rooms behind and a ladder up to a loft. A fire rippled on the hearth, for it had turned off chillish in the night. I saw a cast-iron stove and a sink against one wall. A shelf held rows of old books. There was a big bearskin for a rug, and a table and chairs, and a couple of rockers up beside the fireplace. Over the door was set a pair of six-point deer horns, and across them lay a rifle, an old army Springfield.

"Have seats," Ben Gray invited us. "What went on at that singing?"

Callie told him all about the picking and singing and dancing, and how I'd won the prize for guitar. I had the prize cup in my hand, and now I leaned in my chair and reached it out to her.

"I'd be mightily proud if you took it and kept it, Miss Callie," I said.

Her big blue eyes got bigger. "Oh no, I couldn't do that, John," she said, and I had it in mind that Warren watched me in a funny sort of way. "I couldn't take it from you. You won it fair and square. You're the best guitar picker I've heard in my whole life."

I still reached the cup out. "If you won't take it as a gift, take it as a trade. You can teach me that song about 'Come Over the Bourn, Bessy.' I'd another sight rather have the song than the cup."

She took it then, and sort of cradled it between her little hands. "You truly want to learn that one?" she asked.

"I aim to sing it to a girl I know, named Evadare."

Warren slacked off when I said that. He twinkled his eye at me to show how glad he was to hear tell that I was a-thinking of some other girl than Callie. He put out his hand for the cup and held it to weigh it.

"I say it's made of solid gold," he allowed. "It weighs heavier than lead, like gold."

We all stood up then and came round to look. It was a right pretty cup. It looked to be hammered out all round. Warren turned it over and over.

"No carat mark," he said. "But it's of home manufacture, anyway. I'll swear again, it's of gold." He gave it back to Callie. "Worth hundreds of dollars."

"Then John shouldn't ought to be a-giving it away so free," said Ben Gray.

"I've done already given it away," I told them, "or anyhow traded it away, for that song I'd rather have."

"I'm sure Callie will be glad to teach it to you, John," said Warren, his voice a-sounding happier every minute. "But first of all, I want to talk about the Shonokins." He looked hard at each of us in turn. "The Shonokins were plainly in charge at that program."

"Sure enough?" said Ben Gray, scowling.

"Yes, and I want what help I can get from you, Mr. Ben."

Ben Gray sat back down in his chair next to the fire. By now, I'd had time to see he was the right sort of mountain man, the sort I knew and liked. He wasn't too much older than Warren and me, but he'd seen life, seen lots of it. He was brown-faced from a-working outdoors; he had good teeth and hands and eyes. From a fruit jar he poured us drinks of pale, straw-colored blockade whiskey. I sipped mine and allowed how good I thought it was.

"I'm proud to hear you say so, John." He grinned. "I made it myself."

"Then you've got good reason to be proud," I said back. "A man who does air thing as good as this deserves to be given credit, same as if he's a good blacksmith, say."

"Or builds a good house or grows and harvests a good

crop," added on Warren, and Callie beamed at him for that.

"I do thank you one and all for what you've got to say about this here blockade," said Mr. Ben, "but it ain't all I do, not by a long shot. I grow me vegetables and tobacco and truck them off to sell. And likewise I'm a bee hunter."

"Nair in all my life have I gone bee hunting," I said.

"All right then, let's you and me go out and hunt a couple of bees along about sunup tomorrow," he invited me. "But Jackson here said he wanted to talk some about them Shonokins."

"Yes, sir." Jackson sipped at his drink. "I came here in the first place because my friend John Thunstone said you'd sent him some mention of them."

"Well, they're hereabouts all right," allowed Mr. Ben, and he didn't sound glad to tell of it. "They started a-coming in when I wasn't much past being just a chap. It was after old Dr. Ollebeare died and went to his rest, and folks started to move out of that settlement they'd named Immer. Moved out and forgot their places here; forgot their ownership, and let the places come up for back taxes, and the Shonokins would get hold of them."

"Back taxes?" Warren repeated him. "Did the Shonokins go to the courthouse to get titles to the land?"

Ben Gray studied that for a second. "Can't rightly answer that, Jackson. Maybe somebody appeared to get the titles for them some way, but they got them. Only I stayed on, and three-four others here and there. And the Shonokins have begun to run into me, in the woods mostly, and they try to talk to me about would I sell my place to them. But they talk more about something else of mine they pure down want me to let them have."

"The alexandrite," said Callie.

"What's that?" I inquired him, for it was another new word to me.

"This here is what."

He dug in the pocket of his blue pants and handed something to me.

It was a pretty thing, and no I reckon about that. A jewel like naught I could remember a-seeing my whole life long. It was as big as my thumb and it shone a shiny red, with dark lights in it.

"When the sun's out, it's green," Mr. Ben said. "It changes to this red color by lamplight. I got it when I was away to the war in Germany. My outfit met some Russian soldiers in a little town where our lines sort of touched, and one of them traded this to me for my watch and some iron rations I had. I heard tell from a major that the Russian czars thought there was power in them kind of stones, back when the Russians had czars."

"It was called alexandrite after a czar named Alexander," said Warren, a-taking it in his hand and a-turning it this-away and that. "And you may be right about a power in it. I've heard of mystics, people that are called psychometrists, picking up strong impulses from alexandrites. But why do the Shonokins seem to want it?"

"They've nair come out and told me that. They seem to know I've got it, and they want to buy it a right much. Offered me big money. I allowed that if it's worth that much to them, it's worth that much to me. You see, folks, I don't much value a-being round with them Shonokins, no way."

"Whatever had they done against you?" I asked.

"Oh, nothing much so far. I've reckoned I could take care of my end of whatever they might could try on with me." He looked like as if he meant that thing. "But I'm like Jackson. What I crave to know is, how come them to want it so much?" He shook his head. "One of youins is a-going to have to ask them. They ain't nair told me yet."

"Things were the other way round with Thunstone," said Warren. "The Shonokins tried hard to give him a rather peculiar jewel, and he managed to destroy it. Thunstone connected the matter with something that happened long ago in Connecticut, back in the 1850s, when a woman named Mary Staplies had two brightly shining jewels she said were gods of some savage sort. Thunstone showed me the case in John Taylor's history of old witchcraft trials in Connecticut."

"I've been a-doing some thinking here," I came in to say. "If there's aught to this Shonokin tale that they were here in America before the Indians, there's maybe some justice on their side."

"That's been their argument, again and again," said Warren. "But I keep asking myself, what sinister enchantment are they mixing into it?"

"I've heard it said, air thing that deceives may be said to enchant," allowed Ben Gray.

I looked up at him. "Where did you get that, Mr. Ben?"

"Out of *Plato's Dialogues* yonder." He cut his eye over toward his shelf of books. "Old Dr. Ollebeare gave that one to me when I was just ten years old, a-helping him chop some wood for his hospital fires. I've done read through it, time and time over again."

"I know the passage," Warren told us. "As a matter of fact, Plato was quoting Socrates."

Callie had set the cup on the fireboard above the hearth, and Ben Gray got up and walked over to look at it.

"Enchantment," he said over again. "Why ain't they scared?"

"The Shonokins mostly fear just their own dead," said Warren. "So Thunstone has found out."

"Hark at me, John and Jackson," went on Mr. Ben. "Should we ought to keep this here cup thing, when the Shonokins gave it to John, maybe with something or other wrong in there where we can't make it out?"

"We don't have to pester ourselves about that," I said. "They nair gave it to me. I won it off them fair, for my guitar picking. And Miss Callie is a-going to win it off me fair, to trade for the song she's agreed she'll help me learn."

"I think John has the right of it," spoke up Warren. "Any sort of enchantment should be broken by the exchange."

Callie and I got our guitars and she taught me the song. I could pick the tune right off, and in a while I learnt the words. We sang it verse and verse about, Callie a-singing for the Queen, I for England, like this:

> "Lady, this long space
> Have I loved thy grace,
> More than I durst well say;
> Hoping at the last,
> When all storms were past,
> For to see this joyful day."

And of all the verses Callie sang for the Queen, I liked one the best:

> "Yes, yet must I forgive
> All such as do live,
> If they will hereafter amend;
> And for those that are gone,
> God forgive them every one,
> And his mercy on them extend."

Jackson Warren listened with all his heart and clapped

for us when we finished. I knew well that he wished he could pick and sing along with Callie.

"Folks," said Mr. Ben finally, "we'd better get us some sleep if John and I get up soon in the morning to go bee hunting. John, I've put Jackson up here in our loft, where there's just the one cot bed. How would it be if we made you up a pallet here next the fire?"

"I thank you," I said, "but why don't I just bed down out on the porch? I've slept so much in the open, I've come on to like it."

"If that's what you want, John, but here, let me give you a quilt to go with your blanket. The nights can be airish hereabouts."

I took the quilt and blanket out the door and spread them on the planks. Inside, they blew out the lamp and went off to their own rooms. I pulled off my boots and rolled up in the quilt and blanket. I hadn't long to lie there to wait for what I'd more than halfway expected.

I'd slept, but I woke up quick all over, the way I always do, because I heard the sound of feet. With my ear to the planks of the porch, I heard them a-coming. I sat up and stared out into the yard. There was a bare wash of light from the moon, and I saw three shapes out there.

They stood close up together. I couldn't rightly make them out, only enough to see that there was something mean about them.

Softly they whispered to one another:

"Him?" said one, soft and secret. "No, not him."

"Not him," another repeated the first. "The ones inside. This one is to be kept."

"Not to be killed," muttered the third.

I got up on my bare feet. "What do you all want?" I called to them.

They bunched closer together at that.

"So I'm not to be killed?" I said. "All right then, get out of here. If you don't kill me, I might could kill one of you all."

And, barefoot, I walked down the steps into the yard.

They whipped round and went a-scuttling out of there like thieves caught in a henhouse. A moment later, they were gone amongst the darkness of the trees.

I sat myself down on the edge of the porch and pulled my blanket up round me, for I felt a touch of chill. I tried to look and see if they meant to come back, but nair sign of them.

Hunkered there, I passed the time by a-singing to myself under my breath. I went over all the verses I'd learnt from Callie for "Come Over the Bourn, Bessy." After that, others. One was a charm song I recollected, about "Three Holy Names, Four Holy Saints." Back in my past, I'd known that one to be of good help.

Time went on and on, the way it always does, one minute after another. I dozed now and then, but no more than dozed, for I was on watch.

Finally I saw the stars pale out, yonder to the east, and a little fingery touch of pink where the sun would be a-coming up. Inside, I could hear a racket of dishes, so I got on my feet and pulled on my boots and went in.

III

They were all awake and dressed up and a-doing things to-gether in there. Ben Gray had built up a hearth fire on last night's bright coals. Callie, in a gingham housedress, was at the stove with a big granite coffeepot. Warren had put him on a checked shirt and now he set us out big plastic cups and saucers. All of them gave me good morning. I didn't speak right off about what had gone on in the yard last night.

"I'll root you out some bee gear, John," said Mr. Ben, and went to rummage in a corner cupboard. He handed me a roll of mosquito netting and a big pair of thick canvas gloves, engineer-style, with heavy cuffs to them. "You can roll your sleeves down and pull them gantlets high onto your wrists," he said. "Now, Callie, pour us out some of that there coffee, and I do hope it's stout."

"It's stout all right, Daddy," she said, and it was. Sooty black and powerful for strength. It grabbed hold on my insides the right way.

"Want another cup, John?" Mr. Ben inquired me. "No? All right then, come along. We'll fetch us back some wild honey for breakfast."

He picked him up a sort of squirt-pump thing and an ax and gave me an iron kettle to carry. He and I went out, and then at last I told him, in a few words, about those three things in the yard during the night.

"Shonokins," he said, like a cussword, while we walked

round the house to the back and past a chicken run and hogpen and into a trail in the woods behind. "I swear, John, I've had my possible fill of them. I don't value them no way. There just ain't no luck where they push in with their outlander ways, all their poking round where they ain't wanted. But come along here to my fishpond."

It was a right good one he'd hollowed out where a stream flowed down. "Looky yonder," he said, and pointed with his gloved forefinger. "Them there bees always comes here to get themself a drink. Make ready to follow on."

We watched a few bees where they'd settled down by the waterside. A couple of them took off with a quick zip and so did Mr. Ben, fast, right there on their track. I followed along. We pushed amongst some thick-grown hemlocks and buckeyes and beeches, and then on underneath a big old oak tree that must have been five feet through at the root. Finally he stopped.

"Lost them," he said. "But the thing is to wait right here; there's bound to be another one will pass by directly."

One buzzed along past us right when he said the words, and we took off on the straight line it drew. We came to a little run of water amongst bushes, jumped across, and climbed a rise. Yet another bee went zip over us, like a bullet.

"Yonder we are," said Ben Gray.

He meant the low, broken stump of a rotten old tulip poplar that likely was once as tall as a church steeple. Most of it had fallen away and there were only two or three twisty branches still a-putting out their few leaves. In its belly showed a big, black hole. From off where we were, I saw a stir of bees there, like steam above a hot pot.

"Now's the time to get that there netting hooded on to you," Mr. Ben said to me. "Spread it over your hat and fetch it down all round to tuck into your shirt and then button your collar to hold it snug. That's the way. Now, you've pulled them gloves on snug, too. All right, let's go get it."

He'd put on his own netting and gloves. We walked up on that poplar stump. It stood maybe seven feet high and most of it looked as rotten as punk. The bees came a-buzzing out round us. Some of them lit on the mosquito netting right in front of my face. That close, they looked as big as toad frogs, their legs and wings a-working. Mr. Ben walked to where that hole showed and set up his squirt-pump thing and lighted it somewhere with a match.

"I made this here smoker my own self," he said, above the buzzing of all those bees. "What I got inside it is a mixtry of stuff—tobacco and such things. Now."

He pumped clouds of black smoke into the place. I saw bees come a-tumbling into the open like as if they'd been told their rent had run out. More smoke he pumped and more, puff after puff. It smelled strong and bitter.

"Use that there ax, John."

I set my feet wide apart and slammed the ax into the rotten wood. I cut a notch, another notch. The whole punky stump cut easy, and the chips showed as pale as buttermilk. I heard the stump crack and looked to see which way it would tilt. More whacks into it. It began to go over.

"Look out the way!" yelled Mr. Ben, but already I'd dodged myself clear of the fall of it. Down it slammed, with a sort of screech as it broke open its whole length and popped into two halves. I could see its hollow inside, built full of shiny, brown, dripping combs, square feet of them. Bees crawled over the honey, a nation of bees. Some came a-clouding to light on us, but their stingers couldn't get to us through the nets and shirts and gloves.

"There's enough there to sell for about fifty dollars in

town," I heard Mr. Ben say. "But let's just take us enough for breakfast."

He had a big spoon, and he scooped honeycombs out of the hollow to fill the kettle. "Now," he said, "we're right close on to the old Immer Settlement Trail. We'll take that out; it's an easier way back home."

He led the way across through belts of other trees, a-breaking twigs on the branches air step he took. Bees followed us along a piece, but they pulled back off from us when we got on a footpath amongst heavy thickets. That footpath looked beaten down hard, and I reckoned that it ran as straight as a guitar string, straight enough even to be drawn by surveyors. The second I put my foot on it, I felt a sort of tingle in my blood, like as if something hummed inside me. Not strong, but it was there.

Ben Gray pulled the netting off his hat. "Do you feel something funny, John?" he inquired me over his shoulder.

"I'm glad you mention it, so I'll know I'm not a-using my imagination," I said back to him. "What causes that feeling?"

"I don't rightly know how to answer that. I've only noticed it myself lately."

We tramped on and on, and when we got to his yard and off the track, the tingle left out of me. By then, the sun was up and a-showing through the pines, and I saw for the first time how good the cabin looked. It had been run up by some builder who knew how to build a cabin, and that was a fact—the logs notched so they lay close one above the other, the corners square as a box, the shakes on the roof cut square and heavy. The front yard had summer flowers to grow in it, bunches of white and yellow and blue, here and there like as if somebody had flung them down there by the handfuls. As we came along up the stone-flagged

path to the door, I could smell pancakes and hear them
pop in the skillet.

Inside, Callie gave us a smile. She had a pancake turner
in her hand and was a-putting stacks on plates that Warren
set out on the table. He likewise poured us more of that
good coffee. Beside each stack Callie served a couple of
brown sausage patties. Then we all sat down together and
Mr. Ben said a blessing. We squeezed honey out of the
combs with a spoon and had us as good-tasting a breakfast
as a man could call for. That honey had the tang of sour-
wood to it. The sort of eating that makes you want to go
out in the sun and loosen up and breathe deep, like a
lizard.

"I'll wash up here," said Callie, "and then maybe Jackson will go with me to fetch back the rest of that good
honey."

"No, daughter, you go on now," Mr. Ben bade her. "Me
and John will do these here dishes one time. Youins can
take the Immer Settlement Trail. I broke off twigs to show
youins where to head into the woods."

"All right, but sometimes that trail gives me a squiggly
feeling," said Callie, and she hiked her pretty shoulders to
show what she meant.

"It ain't no far way from here," said Ben Gray, "and
anyway, I'd like for Jackson to see if he picks up that same
feeling while he walks the trail."

The two of them found big hats and draped on the netting, and each of them took two big kettles to pack the
honey in. Out they went, a-talking to one another right fast
and friendly.

We filled a big pan with hot water and Mr. Ben Gray
washed the dishes while I wiped them on a towel made of
a flour sack.

"I got them out of here so we could talk," Mr. Ben said.

"John, what's your idea of this Jackson Warren man?"

"I've only just met him," was all I could reply. "I like him so far."

"Well, I ain't been a-knowing him but a couple days my own self. I reckon him to be all right, a-being as how Mr. Thunstone sent a letter by him to say he was a good fellow. But after all, I got to pay him some mind, the way he seems to like Callie and Callie don't seem to hate him."

He went on to tell me how much store he set by Callie. She'd been a scholar at Flornoy College, a-studying to be a music teacher, but when her mother had died all of a sudden, she'd come right back home to keep house for her daddy. And she seemed to feel happy about that, and nowadays her only music study was the old, old songs of the mountains. It seemed to Mr. Ben that Callie wanted to learn those pretty much the same way I'd always wanted. But about Jackson Warren:

"It's always been my way to make up my mind quick on a stranger," he said. "Decide by just how I feel about him if I'm a-going to trust him as a friend, or either not even talk to him if I ain't got a business reason to. And I ain't much gone wrong on that sort of plan. I liked Jackson Warren from the first five minutes. Now, of course, he's older than Callie. Maybe twelve-fifteen years."

"Sure enough," I said, "and I take notice that he reminds that thing to her, wants her to take it into air thought about him. I call that a-being honest."

"And I agree you there. Well, let's talk about something else. The Shonokins."

While we finished up the last of the dishes and put them away, we talked about the Shonokins. He allowed that they'd been sort of to themselves, off there in that torn-down old settlement of Immer where the folks had left out and the Shonokins had come in. The Shonokins seemed to do all right for themselves there. One place and another they'd even helped some of the folks still a-living round, had cured sickness with plants they knew and the like of that. But he didn't relish what he kept a-calling the "outlander" way they had, and how they wanted to pester him to sell his place, and especially how they went on about that alexandrite stone he always carried with him.

"John," he said, "I aim to leave that jewel stone to Callie when I go. It ain't for the Shonokins."

"Maybe they're up to some good sort of thing," I said, though I didn't much think that as I said it.

"Not them." Mr. Ben shook his grizzled head. "If they're up to aught of good, it's their own good. It's like this: I done told you I liked Jackson Warren right off, because that's a mountain man's way with strangers. But I'll likewise add on to that—I ain't nair liked the Shonokins right off, nor yet as time keeps on."

He dumped the dishwater into his sink.

"Hello, the house!" came a holler from outside.

Mr. Ben tramped to the door and opened it. "Who's out yonder?" he yelled back. "Oh. It's you, Mr. Altic."

Nor did he say to come in. I walked over to look.

Brooke Altic stood on the flagstones. He wore another suit of fancy clothes, a sharp plaid jacket and plaid pants, with a white turtle neck to his shirt. On his hands were pearly-gray gloves, not big ones like what we'd worn to go bee hunting, but drawn snug as his skin. His eyes were hidden behind his dark glasses. His long black hair was as slick as if it had been painted down with a brush. I thought his nose looked sharper than a knife, and his teeth showed white when he smiled them at us.

"Whatever do you want of me?" Mr. Ben inquired him, and he didn't sound as if he'd much give what was wanted.

"Little enough of you this morning, sir." Altic's voice

was as soft and friendly as a summer wind amongst the flowers. "I want only to speak a profitable word or two with the guest you have here. The master guitar player you call John."

"I'll talk to him," I told Mr. Ben Gray, and stepped out on the porch. "Yes, sir, what can I do for you?"

"Suppose you and I sit on the step here." He smiled and smiled. "And let me tell you how I want to make your fortune."

I sat down and so did he. He crossed one leg on the other. The boots he wore were a sort of shiny blood-red, like a berry. I bet myself they'd been specially made and cost a plenty.

"Since last night I've been hearing about you, John, and everything I've heard is greatly to your credit," he said, with a show of his teeth. "I want you to join the winning side in what's due to happen."

"I've always more or less wanted to join the right side," I said back, while I figured on him with those fine clothes.

"In this case, the winning side happens to be the right side," he said. "The side that's due to be proved right by respectable federal law. It concerns the Shonokins. Have you ever heard of the Shonokins, John?"

"Lately I've heard tell two-three things," I replied him.

"I got up early this morning to tell you more things. Morning isn't really the best Shonokin time. After dark, the Shonokins." He studied me. "Perhaps you've been told something about the Shonokin right of ownership of the whole of America; a lawful title that goes back for tens of thousands of years, to times long before the people you call Indians invaded from Asia and seized the land from them?"

"Yes, sir," I said. "I've been a-hearing something along

that line. What you want to say is, the Indians haven't got the first true rights to America."

"Quite ably put," he said, a-studying the shiny toe of his boot. "Of course, the Indians think they have those rights. Just now, they're at law in half a dozen places to prove those so-called rights. It's something rather gigantic, particularly up in the northeastern states, where the old tribal lands are being demanded again."

He started a-telling it off on his fingers. He touched the first one.

"About ten million acres in Maine for the Passmaquoddies and Penobscots." He touched another finger. "More big returns of territory demanded in Massachusetts, for the Mashpees on Cape Cod and the Wampanoags on Martha's Vineyard and other places." Another finger. "Again, for the Pequods and Mohegans and others in Connecticut." Yet another finger. "For the Oneidas and Cayugas and Mohawks in New York State." He'd used up the four fingers on that hand, and touched the thumb. "Here in the South, a big slice of South Carolina for the Catawbas and another slice in Louisiana for the Chitamaches. To say nothing of claims in the Southwest."

He doubled the fist in its gray glove. It looked slim to me. I recollected it could have quite a grip.

"Oh," he said, a-smiling, "I could go on all day about this big list of legal actions. And you and I don't have all day."

"I said I'd heard tell just a little bitty bit about all this," I said. "You seem to be right much informed, Mr. Altic. Right much educated."

"My education isn't formal, but I have something like four thousand books where I live," he said. "I chose each one for its useful information. Very well, John, and what have the Indians to support all these demands, these lawsuits? Why should anyone pay attention to the Indians, anyway?"

"Well," I said, "I haven't air seen children a-playing cowboys and Shonokins."

He laughed at that. It was a sort of crooning laugh.

"You have a perceptible gift of homespun humor, I see. But back to the Indians: All their lawsuits are predicated on the Nonintercourse Act of 1790—one of the early acts of the United States Congress—that recognized certain aboriginal rights of the various tribes."

"I've had that explained to me one time," I said, "by an old Cherokee medicine man named Reuben Manco. President George Washington his own self read the thing out to a bunch of Indian chiefs. And air since that day, the white Americans have been a-breaking that old law, time and time again, and maybe these Indians today have got a something to say for what it is they want. They were here first, on the ground they've just purely been run off of."

"The point is," said Altic, "they weren't here first. They aren't the true, lawful aborigines. The Indians dispossessed the Shonokins."

"And I said I'd been told something about that argument."

"We Shonokins have been pushed into hiding." He wasn't a-smiling then. His maple-colored skin looked tight on his face. "But we've never gone completely away from the land that is rightfully ours. Never."

"You've hidden," I said. "Now you all want to come out of hiding."

"We want to, and we shall." He sort of snapped that out. "The United States Government, I say, is now in a mood to listen to fair arguments at last. To grant fair titles, which is no more than we deserve. The federal law will be on the side of my people."

"Your people," I repeated him. "You talk like the chief of your people. Are you?"

"I'm the chief of those that are here. The chief of us all —but never mind just now who the chief is, or where. Back to the legal aspect as recognized by human justice. Here within recent times, in the case of Montoya versus the United States, the Supreme Court clarified tribal rights and also established a specific definition for the word tribe. It goes something like this: A group of the same or similar race, united as a community under one leadership or government, and inhabiting a particular, though sometimes ill-defined territory. All right, those terms exactly describe the Shonokins."

He talked sharp and stern, but I kept my own voice quiet. I said, "Seems to me I recollect Reuben Manco a-telling those things over to me, too. And he allowed, a tribe meant a people or nation of Indians."

"The Supreme Court offered its definition to consider the specific problems of the Indians," Altic said, back in his smooth-talk way again. "In any case, that word—tribe—is a word of the white man, not the Indian. It comes, as I understand, from the Latin *tribus*—the old Romans recognized people as tribes."

"There may be a lot in what you say," was all I could give him.

"I would also suggest that the word came into your use out of the Bible, where, you'll remember, there were the twelve tribes of the Children of Israel."

I thought to myself, it would be a pure pleasure to hear Brooke Altic talk if I wasn't a-pestering myself to know just what he was a-getting at.

"And," he went on then, "the Supreme Court needs only to be properly informed of the nature of the Shonokins to come to recognize them as a tribal group of their own. Not Indians, not whites. Not, strictly speaking, human as you define human."

"Not human," I said after him, a-trying to understand.

"But, nevertheless, the original and rightful owners of this whole continent that calls itself America after the Italian adventurer who never discovered it."

He gazed through his dark glasses at the flowers in the yard. He didn't seem to think to himself how pretty they were. He just calculated.

"How do you all aim to make folks believe these things?" I inquired him.

"By our antiquities. We'll interest the experts at the Bureau of Ethnology. They can be shown where to dig up Shonokin remains of many millennia of the past."

I looked at him hard. "You'll open up your graves for them?"

"No, John." He sort of squinched his face at the thought. "We'll not open any graves ourselves. They can do the grave-opening and examine the remains and be convinced."

"Convinced?" I repeated after him. "How?"

"By recognizing the special characteristics of Shonokin skeletons. There are interesting racial peculiarities. For one, our third fingers are longer than our middle fingers."

He peeled off his left glove and held out his hand. It was a slim, smooth hand, and again I recollected how strong it could take hold of you. Sure enough, the third finger was the longest. I saw that his nails were narrow and as dark as iron, and came to lean, sharp points. More like claws than nails.

"We'll prove our rights," he said, a-drawing the glove back on and smoothing it to his fingers. "And we'll win our rights."

I was a-thinking all the time. "The way you put things,

the Shonokins would wind up a-running this country and the whole bunch of other folks would be lucky to wind up on a reservation somewhere."

"Would that be so bad, John?" he asked, sort of a-pushing his face at me. "If you were a Shonokin, would that be so bad?"

I got up on my feet. "Only I'm not a Shonokin, Mr. Altic."

He got up, too. He hiked on his toes, a-trying to be somewhere near as tall as I am.

"What if we made you a Shonokin?"

I shook my head. "I don't see how."

"Here and there we've persuaded useful men to join us," he said. "Lawyers, for instance, lately we've needed them. What if we accepted you as a Shonokin, John, important among us?" He pushed his face again. "I could manage that for you. I told you I hold an important position."

"How do you reckon I could help you?" I inquired him.

He held out his gloved hand. "You could start by getting me a certain jewel from Ben Gray."

"No"—and I shook my head—"I can guarantee you that he won't give that up till he's dead."

"Until he's dead? Hmmm." He sounded as dark as his glasses. "By the way, John, that's an interesting belt you're wearing."

"This?" I looked down at it. "Just a plain leather belt."

"I'll trade you mine for it." He pushed open his coat and put his hand to a fancy, shiny buckle. "This is worked in gold—"

"I thank you, but I won't trade," I busted him off. For that belt had been given to me by my true love Evadare. "But tell me, why me?"

He sat down again, and so did I, after a second. "Because you can give us valuable help, John, like the born persuader I see you are. You seem to be able to influence people. You might even influence the United States Government."

"Nair in my life have I thought I could do such a thing," I said.

"Then think of it now." He rocked back and forth where he sat. "We'd send you to the President himself, to make him hear and vindicate us, like another Washington. It would be worth his while. We have things to offer in exchange. Our wisdom is the oldest and greatest on Earth."

"You sure enough make it sound thataway," I had to grant him.

"In these long, secret centuries, we've learned to bring about wonders. We can command life and death. Man has bungled badly. The Shonokins won't bungle."

"Man," I repeated him. "The way you talk, you sound like as if men are one thing and Shonokins another."

"Two different creatures," he said. "Man has descended one way, the Shonokins another. They're similar, but they're distinct."

"Well now, what's the advice you said you'd come to give me?"

"My advice," he said, slow and cheerful, "is to be practical and wise and modest. Don't defy a greater power than hurricanes."

"You reckon I'm not brave enough to challenge you."

"If you did," he said back, "I'd deplore your bad judgment. See here, John, we Shonokins are ancient and great. We had power and wisdom when your forefathers were still wild brutes."

"You want to rule over men," I guessed.

"In a word, yes." He bit that off at me. "Forgive me if I sound blunt, if I don't seem to favor your sort of people. That's because my sort of people hasn't been favored at all, hasn't been considered, for long ages. Now, I've explained the rights and wrongs of the matter, John, and it's up to you to recognize them and tell them apart."

Out reached his gloved hand, like as if to shake mine, but I didn't take it. I got up again and jammed my own hands down into my pants pockets.

"Rights and wrongs aren't all that easy to tell apart," I said to him. "Now and then, it's too hard to rightly tell. But you've done a lavish of talking here. Let me reply you this. You're a Shonokin."

"Yes," he said. "Yes, of course."

"And I'm a man. What I've got to do is stay on the side of men."

He jumped up and flung back his head. "I think you'll change your mind before I'm through with you."

"No, Mr. Altic, because you're through with me right now." My hands made fists in my pockets. "Good day to you."

He replied nair word to that. He turned on the built-up heel of his boot and slammed off fast down the path to the woods. I watched him go out of sight on the track there, then I went back up on the porch and into the cabin.

Ben Gray stood just inside the door. "You don't need to tell me what went on with the two of you," he sort of grumbled. "I was where I could hark at air word of it."

"Then you might could help me figure what he's up to," I said.

"Ain't no need to figure on that. He's up to trouble for us."

"Last night," I reminded him, "there were Shonokins out yonder. I heard them allow I was to be saved for something. But now, I don't rightly expect they'll keep a-figuring on a-saving me, since I've spoken my piece to Brooke Altic."

"Well," said Mr. Ben slowly, "it's still right soon in the morning. But these hellacious goings-on makes me feel I'd just like a drop of blockade to help me a-thinking them over."

He went to his shelf where the glass jar was and put up his hand for it. But he nair took hold of it.

Because just then, another hail sounded outside, a long, sort of mournful one.

"Ben Gray . . . come out; Ben Gray . . . come out."

IV

Mr. Ben took his hand back quick from the jar. "Who's that out there?" he said. "Don't seem to me like I know that voice."

"It's someone who knows you, anyway," I said.

"Ben Gray," called the voice again, sort of mournful to hear.

"We'll soon see," said Mr. Ben. "You wait in here, John."

He crossed the floor and cracked the door out. "Three fellows a-standing yonder. They look like—"

He nair finished that, but went right on out. I stepped to a front window where I could see the yard.

In the strong morning light, I made out three shapes just at the edge of the woods, where that track to Immer started. They wore long, dark coats and low-pulled hats. I'd seen such as that the night before.

Mr. Ben was off the porch and went a-walking down the path toward them. "Who's youins?" he inquired them. "Come on, give a name to yourselves." He was a-walking careful, but he walked at them.

"Stop," said the voice that had moaned his name. The middle one of the three came up with his hand, and it had a long blue pistol in it. "Just stand right where you are," said the voice.

Ben Gray had stopped. I saw his shoulders hunch up.

"Who's youins?" he wanted to know again.

"Never mind who we are," said the one with the pistol. "We've got business with you, Ben Gray. Business with what you always carry in your pocket."

"What you a-talking about?" Ben Gray's hand moved to his side pocket.

"That's right, take it out," bade another voice, a scratchy one. "Throw it down on the cobblestones in front of you."

I saw Mr. Ben draw up his shoulders again. It made him look taller. Then: "No!" he yelled.

And he whipped round, swift as a bird. His feet were a-going as he turned, and he ran back toward the cabin. As he ran, he buck-jumped to the right, then to the left, amongst the pines.

The one with the pistol fired it off. It didn't rightly sound like guns I knew, more of a yelp than a bang. As it sounded, Mr. Ben was out of sight, round the corner of the cabin. I took time to remember there was a gun for me, too, up there on the deer horns over the half-open door. I made a step thataway.

"No, John, let me."

That was Ben Gray. He'd come in through a back door and up to the front of the room. He grabbed down the rifle, that old Springfield. As he dropped down on one knee, he worked the bolt. Up to his shoulder he slammed the stock, and he took aim and fired out through the door.

I'd jumped back to the window. Out yonder, I saw that those three fellows had come halfway along the path. As the rifle spoke, one of them at the right sort of stumbled and wagged his head. The other two looked his way as Mr. Ben fired again.

That time, the one at the right doubled clear over and near about went down. His two mates grabbed hold of him and dragged him, half-falling, back along the path toward the trees and the trail beyond. They made speed at it, for all they had to help him. Ben fired a third time at them, over their heads, and they fairly flew off amongst the summer leaves.

"You nair got done what you come to do, did you?" he howled after them.

The three were gone. Swallowed up by the woods. Mr. Ben dropped the butt of his rifle to the floor with a thump, and kept a-looking out through the doorway.

"You hit one of them," I said. "I could make that out."

"And I hope it wasn't no little slight wound," he said, and he sounded savage. "They opened up on me in my own yard. But now they're gone."

I, too, looked out at the yard. "Likely gone for good," I agreed him. "You recollect that Jackson Warren told us that Shonokins are plumb scared of their own dead."

"Shonokins," he said after me. "You saw they were Shonokins, too."

"They might could have been the same three that tried to visit here last night. Anyway, if the law comes to ask about it, you've got me for a witness you fired in self-defense."

"Shucks, I don't expect the law will air hear tell about it."

From his cupboard Mr. Ben searched out a ramrod and some patches and a little bottle of gun oil. He worked the rifle bolt to eject out the cartridges and sat down by the door to clean the bore.

We heard more voices outside, and both of us jumped up. But it was only Callie and Warren, a-carrying their kettles of honey up the steps and into the house.

"We must have brought back forty pounds of it," said Warren, a-hoisting his load up on the table. "And we didn't get it all, at that."

"We thought we heard gunshots," Callie added on. "Were you shooting at something, Daddy?"

"Yes, daughter," he replied her, calm and quiet. "I was a-shooting at something."

He had finished his job of rifle cleaning, and he fed cartridges into the magazine and put on the safety and hung the thing back on the deer horns.

"Sit down," he said. "Hark at what's been a-going on here while you two went for those loads of honeycombs."

And he related all about Brooke Altic's visit and his offers, which I'd rejected, and about the shooting afterward. Callie gasped and looked scared; Warren paid attention and didn't make a move or sound while Mr. Ben did his talking.

"They mean business," said Warren at last.

"And goddam ugly business," Ben Gray put on to that. "Killing business, if they can handle it thataway. One of them went off a-carrying some lead I slapped into him. If he dies, he'll scare them up a tad, if what Jackson says about a-fearing their own dead is so."

"Likely they weren't so good at a-shooting in the daylight," I offered. "That Brooke Altic fellow said something like that. After dark, the Shonokins, was what he said."

"After dark, the Shonokins," Mr. Ben repeated me. "When they come here in the morning light, they must have reckoned I'd be easy. They found out something another sight different."

"Daylight or dark, this is a place of deadly danger, Mr. Gray," said Warren. "I know you're not a timid man, but if you were to go away—"

"Not me," Mr. Ben broke right in on him. "I'll nair be run off my own land."

"And if Daddy stays, I stay," said Callie.

"And so likewise do I." I put in my own word. "Folks,

to leave out of here now would be to quit to them, give them this place of yours to take over the way they seem to have taken over that old settlement you call Immer. They want it bad, the way they want Mr. Ben's alexandrite jewel, the way Brooke Altic seemed to want my belt. Those things aren't wanted for good, I'll warrant you. I'll be a-staying, even if the rest of you go."

"None of us are going, then," Warren said, and I'll be dogged if he didn't sound happy about it. "I just suggested it; I didn't advise it. But what do we do first?"

We all looked at one another.

"You can give me a gun, Daddy," said Callie. "You taught me how to shoot."

"Yes, I done that thing," he allowed, a-smiling at last. "And you're a good shot too, honey girl."

"I can handle a gun," I said.

"So can I," added on Warren, "though I don't particularly relish them. But, since we're taking stock of things here, let me say how I felt out there on the way to Immer."

He told us that he'd felt a jangle inside himself when he walked that track. He thought it was just only a slight churning in his blood, maybe the sort of thing he'd feel if he was getting a little electric shock, or either the jiggle you have on one of those electric beds in hotels here and there.

"We both felt it as soon as we got on the trail just outside the yard here," he finished up. "It was gone when we went into the woods at the place you'd marked for us to find the honey. When we came back on the trail, the sensation came back, too."

"It's sort of woogey, I think," said Callie.

Mr. Ben hadn't once ceased from his watch out at the door, like as if he expected a Shonokin to show up air second. "It's their doing," he said. "They're a-playing a game with us, and they've got it in mind they hold a good hand in it. But I'd say we've got a few cards our own selves."

Mr. Ben went into his room at the back and fetched out guns. He gave Warren a deer rifle, and Warren took hold of it like a man who knew how to handle it. For Callie, Ben Gray had fetched out an old army carbine, the kind that's light and easy to use and mighty true to the mark inside two hundred yards. He had a rifle for me, one that looked German, as I thought; but I set it in a corner.

"I've been a-studying," I said to them. "That track outside yonder, that stretches so straightaway from here, with the hummy jingle it gives the blood—I've got it in mind to go out and follow it to where it goes."

Mr. Ben's jaw dropped about a foot. "You want to go to where all those Shonokins hang out?"

"That's exactly where I want to go," I replied him.

"John, that would amount to supererogation," Warren argued at me. "If you know what I mean."

"I know what you mean; I've heard the word used. It means a-doing more than you're called on to do. I'm a-calling on myself to do it."

I started for the open door. Ben Gray got in front of it.

"Hark at me, John, and it'll be water on your wheel to pay me attention. I done heard that Brooke Altic a-talking to you. The way you talked back, he's more than likely figured you'd be better out of his way, same as he figures on me."

I shook my head. "Just now, they count on me a-being here. They'll look for me here, not there. And anyway, somebody's got to find out what they're a-fixing to try."

I moved at the door again, and this time he cleared the way. As I walked out on the porch, I thought I heard Callie sort of gasp, but I didn't look back. Down the steps I went, and along the flagstone path where the three Sho-

nokins had tried to make Mr. Ben fling down his alexandrite.

I came to a place with a show of blood. It was a scatter
of dried red specks in the grass, more or less like any blood.
That was where Mr. Ben's bullet had ripped into one of
the Shonokins. I stepped across it, paced along to the edge
of the yard, and just beyond I saw the track where, they all
said, it would lead you to the old Immer settlement.

I stopped before I set my foot into that track, and
looked off along it. It led northwest, more or less, and
again I noted how straight it ran. Like a string drawn tight,
like a foot ruler many, many feet long; like, well, like the
way those bees had flown earlier in that morning, zip, a
line drawn through the air, a beeline. It looked hard-
pressed down, like as if a many feet had walked it, and it
went to where the trees hid it yonder.

I stepped onto it, and right that same second I felt the
hum in me, the little quiver in my blood. It was like a
warning signal to go back. I didn't go back. I took off on
the way, toward wherever it would lead me.

Trees, there were trees a-growing to each side, thick as a
snake fence. I knew those trees, I saw oak, hickory, short-
leaf pine, locust, beech, all kinds. Thick they grew there in
their green summer leaves. They were so thick there might
could have been an army a-hiding behind them either side,
all ready to jump out at whoever walked that path. Under-
foot, the ground was as hard as stone, like as if it had been
tromped flat. Here and there showed a little tag of moss,
but mostly just the ground. Dark ground, with the drop-
pings and rottings of long years of leaves and twigs. It
would be rich, that ground, rich to grow a garden. But the
hardness of it would blunt the share of a plow, it seemed
like to me.

Up ahead, where the close-grown trees had blotted out

the track, they opened up as I walked toward them. Beyond I could see more of the way I'd chosen to walk. Always drawn as straight as a line made with a straight-edge. And always, the tingle in my blood, the hum there. I stepped off to the side once, to see what would happen. The tingle left off; stepping back, I got it with me again.

This was something special, I told myself as I felt it, this was a thing I'd never felt before, never dreamed before. Maybe it was a Shonokin thing, put on here to keep ordinary folks off this trackway. But how did it work?

Not a-knowing how, I quit the study of it the best way I could, and looked on ahead.

Always up ahead, the straight, hard track, straight, straight. I kept a-walking it, the way I'd vowed I would. The jangle stayed in me, made my ears ring like silver bells. It got stronger, stronger. I wondered why. I could stand it, though, and I kept on my way till I came to where I saw rocks piled up in a clear space by the track side.

They were a great big rock on a little one, and, gentlemen, I mean that great big rock was great big. The bottom one was maybe the size of a dishpan turned upside down, and on it was set a round boulder that must have been six feet through. I reckoned it would weigh tons. It would have taken a derrick to set it thataway. I stopped there to look, while my blood and belly and ears jangled.

That boulder had a ribbed, green look that reminded me of some sort of a melon. I couldn't rightly say what kind of rock it was, though I mostly know the rocks I see as I wander the mountains. The one it stood on, or balanced on, was a dark, slaty kind, such as sometimes a man will break off into chunks to make a foundation for his house or barn. Whatever did they mean, I wondered myself, and who'd set them up there, and when? I put out my hand to touch the big top rock.

And quick I took my hand away again, the way you'd pull back from a-touching a hot stove. That boulder had sent a stabbing shock through me like electricity. As I stepped away, I saw that it bobbed, swayed back and forth, so much, I wondered if it would come off the little underneath rock and maybe roll on me.

If it had, I couldn't have got myself out of its way. I stood where I was, like as if roots had come out of my boot soles and grown down into the ground. I hate as much as the next man to admit a-being scared, but right then I was. Somebody who says he's nair been scared likely nair came up against something to scare him.

I watched that big old darnick of a boulder sway itself at me, back away from me, at me again for maybe six seconds before I jumped back on the hard-pounded trail and sort of ran crookedly there to get clear. I took up my journey once more. The stir in me fell off a little bit, and I looked behind me as I walked. The boulder was still a-rocking from my touch on it. I didn't look back again as I went on ahead.

After all, the way I told myself, there were other balanced rocks in this world. I'd heard tell of them in England, quite a good few there. And there was one in the Chimney Rock part of these very mountains where I was, and a right big one somewhere in the Colorado mountains. You could come on such things. The only point was, such balanced rocks were usually one and the same with the chunks they balanced themselves on. And this one was another sight different from the piece underneath.

Which, I figured as I kept on a-going, meant it must have been put there by somebody, by the hands of somebody. Put there for a purpose. What purpose?

I couldn't reply myself on that. I felt right glad that I'd left the thing behind just now, and that the jangle in me had gone quieter. Felt glad, till I reminded myself that I'd meet up with it again on the way back. But all right, I'd decide on that when I came back. Just now I'd do what I'd said I'd do, go on to the settlement they'd once called Immer, the settlement where the Shonokins were supposed to be. I came to a stream, narrow but fast-flowing, right across the track. I jumped it.

After dark, the Shonokins, that's what Brooke Altic had said to me. I was glad that the sun kept a-climbing and a-climbing, with now and then a patch of it amongst the trees. That was a comfort to me, and right about then I sort of needed comfort.

I tried to reckon how long I'd been on the way. I hadn't brought a watch; I don't often have one. I looked up at the sun—it wasn't much up from when I'd started, probably no more than twenty minutes' worth. Usually I do a mile in better than that time, but then I'd stopped a little while to study the balanced rock. I decided to make my trip so far a mile's way.

And as I went on for what might could be the start of another mile, I kept a-watching the trees to left and right. They were the same trees as before, but there was difference in there with them. They were grown up, across from one another, with vines. And not only ivy and honeysuckle and woodbine; another kind of vine, new to me who'd always watched such things. It was a knotty-looking thing, with round leaves so dark as to look almost black, and blossoms on it with pale milky petals and out of each a red scrap like a tongue stuck out at you.

I didn't like that kind of flower, and I kept my feet on the track that seemed to keep its quiver in my blood.

Then I came to a stop again.

A sort of shallow ditch went down at the side of the

track. In it lay a quiet somebody, a somebody that didn't move, that wouldn't move again in this world.

I bent to look. Sure enough, a Shonokin. I could tell that by the long black coat he wore, by his long, snaky black hair, and by one outflung hand that had a third finger longer than the middle one.

He was dead. I've seen enough dead things in this life to know death when it lies there before me. I bent closer but I didn't touch him. His lips were dragged back and I saw his clenched teeth, small and narrow and grubby-looking. He was bloody in two places, the chest of his black coat and the side of his neck above it. Ben Gray's two rifle shots, I told myself. Mr. Ben didn't mess round when he aimed at you and pulled the trigger.

And the Shonokin's two friends had got him that far along, and then just went off and left him. He must have died right there, and they'd dropped his body and let it lie. It must be the truth what Jackson Warren said—nothing threw a scare into Shonokins like their own dead. That would be why the old-timey Indians had whipped them in war; Indians, even far back then, were bound to be good killers with spears and arrows and tomahawks. I stood a-looking down at that poor dead Shonokin who'd scared his own kin so bad.

But there was nothing I could do for him now, so I went on ahead.

Along a little way farther, I thought for a second I was a-coming to the end of the straight track. Then I saw that wasn't so—it just came to a big hike in the ground and went up over. I walked to the place and stopped to figure. Why hadn't they run their trail to right or left, where the ground was easier? The Shonokins must know the answer, but I didn't. I went up the trail over the hump, and it was so steep I almost had to go on my all fours. I reckon I had to go eighteen-twenty feet to get to the top, twice my height above the track if you measured straight up.

When I got there, I saw the settlement that had been Immer.

The trees thinned out round it, so I could see houses. Only they didn't truly look any great much like the houses built by folks, by people like us, by men.

V

And that settlement once named Immer was way back beyond, at that; it was sort of closed in most of the way round by a laurel hell, grown up so thick and matted together you'd figure a man might could get up and walk on top of it. If you don't mind, you can push into a laurel hell and get so trapped you'll nair get out again. In the open space stood a couple dozen houses, if they were sure enough houses.

For one thing about it, there wasn't what you could call a straightaway street. That wondered me, when I thought how dead straight had run the track I'd traveled. The houses, such as they were, stood in little circles of ground for yards. Paths curved round the circles, onto paths round other circles for other houses. I reckoned a man had better know where he'd be a-going from one part of the settlement to the other. But the Shonokins must surely know, and men didn't belong there.

I walked down the other steep side of the rise, and stepped off the track where it came to its end. Right when I did that, the humming and jangle left out of me, and I was glad of their going.

I stood there and studied the houses. No movement amongst them, nor in the dark patches that might could do them for windows. No smoke went up from the houses. When it comes to that, I saw naught on air roof that looked like a chimney. I made out growing things in the yards, but those weren't plants like what I'd air seen before; and I recollected that vine that had grown beside the track, the one with the unchancy flowers. Though there were flowers on some of these plants. I stood and studied.

Chiefly there seemed to be sort of shrubby growth. I was close in enough to the nearest house to make plants out. They had thick, slobby leaves with red veins, like as if blood flowed in them. What at first I'd thought were blossoms had more the look of tags of pink meat, more or less hand-shaped. The breeze stirred them, I told myself; but just then there wasn't a breeze, so they must be a-stirring of their own notion. They had spiky edges like fingers, that halfway opened and then halfway closed like sure enough fingers.

I didn't feel a call to come too close to such things, a-growing there in clumpy beds. Because I had the notion that they might could get hold on you like real hands; drag you down, even. And then what? Eat you? Gobble you up, like as if you'd fallen into a penful of mean hogs? I couldn't reply myself exactly, though I had ideas—scary, chilling ideas. Plants like that had the look of something able to suck the blood out of you and then the meat off your bones. Who knew, who could rightly say? Maybe them it had happened to were past all saying about it.

Here and there such things grew up, up above the rest of them, taller than a man. Almost like trees. On them, the hand-flowers hung down and looked ready set to grab hold of aught within reach.

That nearest house, amongst plants like that and others near about as strange, was more or less a plumb ruin to see. It looked bent thisaway and that by time's heavy hand, though when it came to that the folks hadn't left out of Immer so many years back. I put my eyes on the house. It didn't show logs in the building of it; it was smooth, like brown plaster. What had at first look seemed to be shingles on the roof weren't like the shingles I rightly knew. More like flattened-out lumps, to remind me of the lichens you see a-growing out on dead trees and rocks. They could have been some kind of wood slabs, they could have been grass bundles, or either something else. And the whole roof, instead of squared-off lines, had a sag to it, a roundness to the edges of it, more or less like the cap of a toadstool. And, as I've said, no chimney on it. The windows weren't like windows, either. More like eyes, drooped under crossbars like eyelids. Secret eyes you can't see into.

But no movement, not a flick of it whatsoever, that I could make out round the houses or in the yards. I had a lone feeling right then, like the last man left on earth. I made myself walk on closer.

In the nearest yard I could make out other sorts of plants beside those bushes with the hand-flowers. On the ground there looked to be little blades of stuff, no bigger than the tines of dinner forks. Then, a row of stalks like corn, but with clusters on it instead of ears, purplish-colored. And, twined round the stalks, vines with fruit, pure down strange-looking fruit, all shapes and sizes.

The house, I made out to see by now, didn't have a true door, just a sort of drape hung there, of what dark stuff I couldn't make out. If I walked to it, I could push it aside easy and go on in. But I wasn't about to do that.

For I recollected, right clearly, tales I'd heard about the sort of house not made with hands. You can come across it here and there in lonesome places, the thing they call a gardinel. I can't tell you where that name comes from, what language or meaning it is. It grows up somehow to house size, they say, and it's there to hope some man will think it's a house sure enough and go in and not come out again.

Because gardinels eat men, so I'd heard tell.

But Shonokins—Brooke Altic had said they weren't true men. Did Shonokins go into gardinels?

"Good morning to you again, John."

It was like as if the thought of him had called him up. Yonder came Brooke Altic, in another suit of his bright, sharp city clothes and his dark glasses; yonder he came round one of those curvy paths to meet me. In one of his gloved hands he toted a cane of polished black wood, with a silver knob at one end and a sharp silver spike to the other.

"So you did come," he said, with his teeth all there in a gleam in his smiling mouth. "I hoped you would. I more or less expected you would."

I stood and looked him up and down, from his grinning face to his polished boots and back, before I answered. "I just sort of thought I'd come along and see what your settlement was like," I said.

"We wanted you to come."

"No, it was my own idea," I told him, while I wondered myself what he'd be up to with me.

"Was it?" Still he smiled. "Very well, maybe it was partly your idea and partly ours. We know ways of using your own thoughts and fancies to get something from you."

I watched that silver-headed, silver-spiked stick of his. Its tip was sharp enough to stab, if so be a man would want to stab.

"You said you expected me here," I reminded him. "Expected me here to do what?"

"To see wisdom. Recognize profit. And now you're here."

I looked again at that nearest house, with its eye-windows, its draped door.

"Go on," Brooke Altic bade me. "Go on in. There's no danger."

"No danger feared, but I won't go in where I don't reckon I'm wanted." I stood with my feet apart, and tried to act as easy about things as he did. "Mr. Altic," I said, "you can just call me a truth seeker. I'd admire to know the whole truth about you Shonokins."

"But I've already tried to tell you some things," he said. "And I've tried to reach peaceable terms with you."

"Peaceable terms," I repeated after him. "Peaceable like those three Shonokins that came with guns after Mr. Ben Gray, to rob him and maybe kill him?"

"They weren't sent after you, John."

"One of them nair made it back to here," I said. "He's a-laying back on that straight, straight track of yours, where his friends left him to lie. I wonder myself if I shouldn't go bury him, a-seeing you Shonokins don't seem to have much mind to it."

"I was told he fell, but I didn't hear where." He didn't seem to let on to feel aught of sorrow for the death of one of his own kind. "But you say you came here to know the truth. Truth about what?"

While he was a-saying that, he walked toward the yard of the nearest house. I walked along beside him. Again I saw the things, the strange things, that grew in the yard. The hand-flowers on the bushes had flecks and streaks of deeper color in their pink, like a sort of orangey brown. And they stirred and half opened, then half shut again.

On the ground grew the little blades I'd noticed, but they weren't grass as at first I'd thought. They looked tight and a lively green.

"You can eat those shoots," said Altic to me. "When you chew them, it clears your mind for better thinking. It nourishes your body for whole days of effort."

He stooped down and tweaked off a couple and chewed them. I didn't do likewise. Instead, I looked at the fruity clumps on other plants.

"Go ahead, eat some of those," Altic invited me. "They're like wine to the taste. And they can cure sickness, almost any sickness."

"I thank you, but I'm not ailing," I said. I looked at more of the houses, farther back. "Where's the rest of your crowd?"

"Resting quietly in their homes, or perhaps busy with certain affairs. John, I wonder at you. You came almost two miles to get here, but all of a sudden you're not curious enough to do any investigating."

"Almost two miles," I repeated him, for that had been near about what I'd guessed the distance to be. "Two miles, dead straight over the face of the land."

"Naturally," he said, a-looking at me through his dark glasses.

"No," I said. "Not naturally, Mr. Altic. Because a straight line isn't natural. And anyway, a track usually turns and bends back and forth, to follow the best, easiest ground for it to run."

He smiled his smile. "But straight lines are indeed natural. Think about it. A beam of light is perfectly straight. The fall of an object, by the law of gravity, is straight."

I thought back on the flight of those bees Mr. Ben and I had traced that morning—shoo, was it just that morning? So much had been a-happening since. There might could be a lot in what Altic said. I turned from him and headed back for where I'd left the track. He strolled along beside me, a-swinging his polished black cane.

Right all of a sudden I didn't want to be round him much, not that I'd truly wanted to from the start. I reached the track and headed back along it. Right away, the jangle came back in my blood and nerves. He moved to come alongside me, he moved right well, like a man in good shape. I sort of wore my way up that steep rise, and at the top he was with me.

"Now, suppose we pause up here a second," he said to me. "I don't think I have to ask you if you experience a certain interesting sensation."

"There's a hum or a shake inside," I said. "It was with me all the way here."

"Now look at this."

He jammed the silver point of his stick down hard. It drove into that packed ground. He let go of the knob and looked at it, a-smiling. I saw the thing begin to bob back and forth, slow at first, then faster.

At first I thought he'd sort of sprung it with his hand to make it do that. But then I made out that it moved of its own self. And it moved strongly. First it whipped one way, then back the other. Maybe like the pendulum of a clock. Maybe like something moved by electricity.

"Do you see the proof of power here?" Altic inquired me.

"Whatever makes it do thataway?"

Always his smile beneath the dark glasses that hid whatever might could be in his hidden eyes. "I doubt if I have the ability to tell you what, or if you have the ability to understand if I do tell you."

"I've seen a water witch with his forked stick, and it bobbed like that. Anyway," I said, "you might could try me on for understanding you. I'm interested in how you talk, air minute. I nair heard a man talk quite like you. What you say about Shonokins."

"I've already told you that Shonokins aren't men." He smiled above the bobbing stick where it was stuck in the ground. "Maybe that puts a speculation into your mind, as to what or whom I might actually be." He pulled the cane out and tucked it under his arm and turned his glasses back to look at me. "I wonder," he said slowly, "if you're turning to one of your quaint human beliefs in a certain old personage who tempts mortals."

I went down from the rise and along the track, and again Altic walked with me.

"I reckon what you're a-getting at is, do I think you're the Devil," I said.

"If you've thought that, you flatter me." He twiddled his cane to and fro. "Your Devil is supposed to have a most impressive manner and a courtly way of talking. But no, John, I'm not the Devil."

"You make me glad to hear you say so," I said. Though I hadn't suggested that he was aught like that, nor yet I hadn't truly thought it.

"You flatter me, I think."

"The Devil," I said as we walked along the humming, jangling way. "He's always a-being told about when he tries to win somebody's soul."

"Ah, there you have it, John," he said, right cheerfully. "We—the Shonokins—have never been prepared to admit the existence of souls."

I just shook my head over that, because I couldn't imagine not to have a soul. I gave him a glance out of the side of my eye. His clothes were fine clothes, and no question at all. I'd nair had such. I didn't expect to be that finely dressed, not even when I married Evadare. I felt shabby, in my old pants and boots and hat, the sort of things I'd wear to go out and work in the field.

"Belief in the soul calls for faith," he said. "A particular religious faith. And we—we're more concerned with proofs. Material proofs. For instance, I'm not only not the Devil; I don't believe in him."

"That should ought to comfort you, Mr. Altic," I said.

He laughed. "You said that you liked to hear me talk. All right, I like to hear you talk. You're highly original and, if I weren't pretty much on my guard, you'd be highly persuasive."

We walked along together. I felt the tingle in my blood.

"Anyway, John," he said at last, "this little stroll you've taken with me must have begun to convince you that the Shonokins are a curious people and not without interesting powers. And I've made you some attractive offers, on which by now you might ponder with some profit to yourself."

Devil or no Devil, Brooke Altic could purely talk well. I kept a-walking along with him.

"What is it you want me to do for you?" I inquired him finally.

"Ah," he said. "Ah, at last. You're beginning to see reason. All right, I wish you'd begin by getting hold of that jewel Mr. Ben Gray carries in his pocket."

"The alexandrite," I said. "What you sent three Shonokins to get from him, and they nair got done what they came to do."

"Yes," he said. "If we could have that—and now we'll have it. You will help us."

"Hold on now," I said, quick. "I just only inquired you what you wanted me to do for you. I didn't say I'd do it."

I started in to walk faster, but he kept up, easily, a-swinging his cane.

"You're beginning to irritate me," he said gently, "and irritating me isn't going to help either of us. You came to our settlement, you say, to find out something about us. And I'm telling you about us. What are you looking at, up ahead there?"

"Naturally you don't know. Come along and see for yourself."

We didn't either one do aught of talking while we slogged along to where we reached the place where that dead Shonokin lay in the ditch where he had been flung.

Altic came on up behind me and looked, too. I heard his breath draw itself in, sharp and scared.

"No!" he sort of burbled. "No—"

And with that, he whipped round in the half of a second and headed back toward his settlement. I watched him go. He flew, almost. His feet looked fuzzy, they were a-moving so fast. Altic was a runner, and that was a pure natural fact.

He went a-plunging out of sight where some tree branches grew down, and I was left alone with that body that lay so still, and I looked down at it.

As I did so, I had a feeling, or rather I missed a feeling. No jangle in my blood, in my nerves, right there. The power, whatever it was, didn't work where the body was.

I bent, but didn't touch it. It lay on its back, with its wide hat down over a face gone as pale as candle wax. The hands were flung over the chest, and I reckoned the dead one's friends hadn't done that, the hands had just fallen there. One sleeve was twitched up. The skin of the arm looked funny. Not true hair on it, only a fine down. I swear, the down had a rib to it, like fluff feathers on a baby bird.

I'm honest to say, I felt a mite sorry for the poor thing. In that moment I felt sorry for all things that had to die in a fight. The war I'd seen, what I did see of it, had taught me how senseless it was to kill or be killed, how war brought closer the end of the world. I looked at the dead Shonokin as he lay flung out. I didn't feel like laying him any straighter, but I felt like a-doing something for him.

Right at that point the ditch was scooped out deep, like

as if something had bit a chunk out of the ground and then spit out the dirt on the far side. I shoved at that pile of dirt with my booted foot. Clods fell in on the Shonokin's body. I more or less covered him up thataway, not deep but at least enough to hide him, not leave him there in the open with his own sort afraid to do it for him. All the time, I wondered myself why I was acting the gravedigger. I thought a second I might could say a prayer, but then I recollected how Altic said the Shonokins didn't believe in the soul. Finally I picked up some rocks and laid them on top of the dirt. Then I took off along the jangly trail, that jangled more weakly than it had done.

I hadn't made many steps before I inquired myself, with that body covered up out of sight, might could not the Shonokins lose their fear, come a-following after me? I took a look back, but no movement on the track, and I kept ahead, hard and dead straight on the dead straight way, with less twinge and stir in me. I moved right fast.

The quivering jangle came up in me again. I reckoned I was a-getting near to that balanced rock. And sure enough, I was, and somebody else stood there next to it.

VI

That quick, I jumped off to where some rocks lay in a bunch, and I grabbed up a chunk of quartz as big as my fist. If a Shonokin was there to give me trouble, I'd feed him back enough trouble to satisfy him a long time. But— next instant, I saw it wasn't a Shonokin, no such thing.

It was only Jackson Warren, and he didn't wear that long coat and wide hat I figured meant the Shonokin kind. He had on the country clothes he'd worn earlier to go a-looking for honey, and his head was bare. He stood yonder to study the balanced rock, like as if it was the Washington Monument and he was a-seeing it for the first time in his life.

"Hey!" I hollered him, and he turned round to look at me, while I made my way to him.

"Whatever's brought you here?" I inquired him.

"I followed you," he said back. "I couldn't let you risk it out here all alone." His eyes were wide and shiny. "Careful, John, don't touch that balanced stone. There's a shock in it that will almost knock you down."

"I found that out already, the hard way," I said. I kept hold of my lump of quartz. "Stand off from it, and off the track."

He moved clear, and I flung the chunk I had. It hit the balanced rock. It teetered thisaway, then back again, and I felt its strong current go through me. We watched while it slowed down its motion.

"I've been to what used to be Immer Settlement," I said. "All the Shonokins there seemed to be a-sleeping by day. All but Brooke Altic."

"Altic?" His eyes crinkled. "Where is he?"

"He came along this track with me, but he got scared back the way he came, by the sight of one of his own dead. I reckon that's the Shonokin Mr. Ben Gray took down with a shot this morning."

Warren drew his mouth tight. "You went all the way? All the way to the settlement? How far, John?"

"I figure about two miles."

"Two miles?" he repeated me.

"Not more than that, as it seemed to me."

"No more than that?" he repeated me again.

"So far as I can reckon by the walk I made. Why? Is it important?"

"It could be. But I'll have to look at some references before I go into that."

He swung round and headed the way to Ben Gray's. "Let's get out of here," he said, in a hushed-down voice. "I touched that balanced stone, and it rocked back and forth like a shirt blowing in a high wind. And it made me feel as if I was being electrocuted."

Together we headed along the track, with that tingle in us. It came into my mind that now the tingle didn't truly hurt. It even seemed to make my feet pick up better. It did me good, sort of.

"I'm getting a theory about this straight travelway," Warren said. "One that will interest you, I think. But I'll not talk about it until we're back at the Gray cabin and I can dig out a book that possibly will fill us in."

We marched along, side by side. Warren looked calmer by now; his face wasn't so paled out. I talked to him about how those houses at the settlement had looked, and the strange things that grew in their yards, and Brooke Altic's new line of talk which I hadn't harked at to buy aught of it.

"He says he's not the Devil, but he's up to deviltry," said Warren when I'd finished. "He's a wrong guy, John. He more or less told you he'd sent those Shonokins to rob Mr. Gray of his jewel, maybe kill him for it."

"Yes," I said, "he did. But they nair got it done."

"Whatever he means to do, he's only started to do it."

We came to where the trail ended. "All right," I said, "here's the house. Who are those men a-talking to Mr. Ben?"

We stepped out of the tingly track into the yard. A gray sedan was parked beside the old car Warren drove. Mr. Ben stood on his bottom step. Two fellows were there together. They wore big wide hats and I saw badges on their tan shirts. One of them said something, and Mr. Ben snapped back at him. We walked up close enough to hear.

"If youins is here today to worry me about blockading," he told them, "go on. Look round my place if you have a mind, see if you can find a still."

"Oh, we ain't interested in no still you might could have," said the biggest of the two. "We ain't a-studying no blockade where you're concerned. What we tried to tell you was, your neighbors allowed there was some shooting a-going on here at your place, so we just thought we'd drop by and—"

"I fired a shot at some kind of varmint was right here in my yard," Mr. Ben broke him off sharp. "I've yet to hear there's a law of the land that says I can't do that. How come you to be here so quick about it?"

"We just happened to be in these parts," said the biggest man. "Heard tell, and come over."

"Heard tell from what loose-jawed talker?" Mr. Ben growled.

"Let's just call that classified information."

While that talk went on, Warren and I came along. The other man turned round to look at us. He was a youngish fellow, pudgy and rosy-faced. He grinned.

"As I live and draw breath," he said, "if it ain't John. How you come on, John, and what you up to in these here parts?"

I knew him then; Dode Griffith, a fairly smart deputy sheriff, who'd now and then been to play-parties where I'd picked and sung.

"Howdy, Dode," I said. "Me? Oh, I'm just a-passing a little time here, on a visit with Mr. Ben."

The other deputy knew me, too. "Glad to see you, John," he said. "So you're a-staying with Mr. Gray here? We just come over to inquire him a few things about some shooting was heard round here."

"It was like Mr. Ben was a-telling you just now," I said. "He saw something sort of dark over at the edge of those trees yonder, and he took a couple of shots and it ran off from here."

"Was you round here when it happened, John?" asked Dode Griffith. "Did you get a look at what it was? It wasn't no man, was it?"

"No," I replied him. "I didn't see it at all clear, but it wasn't aught human. I can guarantee you that."

"A bear, maybe?" wondered the big deputy.

"No," I told him. "At least, I couldn't rightly call it a bear."

Mr. Ben's mouth tightened up under his grizzly moustache. "All right, will John's word satisfy you fellows?" he wanted to know.

"John's word sure enough satisfies me," allowed Dode Griffith, and nodded his head.

"And it satisfies me, too," said the other deputy. "When John here says something, it should ought to satisfy air man who knows John."

Mr. Ben toned down a trifle. "Then all right, folks," he said, some friendlier. "Since that's been settled with youins, come on in the house and have some coffee with us. I'd even offer you a grain of blockade if there was such a matter here round my place."

Both the deputies laughed at that, the way you'd think it was a big joke, and at last Mr. Ben laughed, too. Things had turned friendly right about then.

"No, sir, we do thank you," said Mr. Dode Griffith. "We got a couple other things to look into round this here part of the county, so we'll just go along and look into them. Good day to you, gentlemen."

The two of them walked off and got into their car and backed out and drove off away. Mr. Ben sort of glittered his eyes after them till they'd rolled plumb out of his sight.

"John," he said then, "I've got you to thank for how you headed them off from how they was a-nosing round. And you done the thing by a-telling them the truth—it wasn't no man I shot at, not a sure enough man."

"Well, not quite the truth," said Warren, like a lawyer in court.

"No, sir, not quite," I agreed him. "I've heard say somewhere that a lie told half the truth is ever the blackest of lies. But I reckon it had to be told thataway, friends. This business we're into here isn't just ordinary business. Mr. Ben, the Shonokins aren't true human folks; aren't men, and if you shot one it wasn't like to shoot a man.

"I wonder if I hit him hard," said Mr. Ben, like as if he dreamed.

"Hard and plumb center," I said.

Mr. Ben sort of glowered off into the woods, the eastward way from that strange, straight track.

"The only neighbor I got close enough to hear me when I shoot is that low-flung, common Sim Drogus," he said. "He ain't got business of his own to tend to, not enough anyways. I'm in a mind to go over talk to him, and I'd be a right unpleasant visitor to his door."

"Would he even be within earshot, sir?" inquired Warren. "Does he stay home all the time?"

"Near about all the time," said Mr. Ben. "Sim Drogus has got the first nickel he air earned. Likewise the second and third and hundred and third and all the rest. And he sits round home and counts them nickels, when he ain't a-listening with them long ears of his." He looked the other way, toward where the Shonokin settlement was. "Whatever the Shonokins might could be up to, yonder," he said, "I've got it in mind to go see Sim Drogus."

"We have a few things to talk about right here," said Warren. "Let's see to them."

"Well, come on in and youins can tell me what it's all about," Mr. Ben said. "Anyhow, the sun's all up the sky to where we can take us a little thimbleful of how-come-you so."

We followed him in through the door. Callie was inside there, where she'd been a-harking at all the talk that had gone on outside. Mr. Ben's rifle leant right beside the one he'd given me.

"Mr. Ben," I said, "just now I've got the idea we can relax us a trifle bit. The Shonokins aren't apt to push us much by the light of the day—even if there wasn't aught out there on their track to slow them up."

"What's there?" Mr. Ben wanted to know.

"A dead Shonokin."

"Oh," he said. "Oh."

"Let's sit down where we can watch out the window," I said, "and I'll tell you two-three things I ran into out there."

He poured us short drinks of blockade and I told about my walk, a-putting in some stuff I hadn't touched on when I told the thing to Warren. I made a point about the dead Shonokin, and how Altic acted scared of it. Warren listened again like as if it was all he had to do in life, and he kept asking me questions. Again and again, he wrote things on paper.

"You tell us again, the way to Immer is straight as a bowstring, and it isn't as much as two miles long in your estimation," he said at last. "Let me go get a certain book your story keeps bringing to my mind. It's in my luggage."

He headed up into the loft where Mr. Ben had bedded him down, and came back with the book. It had a green paper over the dark cover of it. He looked at the back and then leafed through.

"Here we are," he said, with his finger on a page. "A quotation from Eliphas Levi."

"Elephant who?" said Mr. Ben.

"Eliphas Levi, Daddy," Callie said the name right. "He was a French scholar more than a hundred years ago. I heard about him when I was at college."

"His real name was Alphonse Louis Constant," Warren told us. "Aleister Crowley claimed to be a reincarnation of him. If that's so, Levi's great sense of humor didn't accomplish the transmigration—Crowley could be awfully pompous and heavy-handed."

He studied the page. "This is the passage," he said. "It's translated by A. E. Waite. It's a formula for bringing the dead to life."

He handed the book to me and pointed the place out. I read the thing out loud:

". . . he must retire at a slow pace, and count four thousand five hundred steps in a straight line, which means following a broad road or scaling walls. Having traversed this space, he lies down upon the earth, as if in a coffin, and repeats in lugubrious tones: 'Let the dead rise from their tombs!' "

Warren took the book back and shut it. "That's all," he said, "except that Levi advises his readers never to try it. Did you hear that it said four thousand five hundred steps?"

"Loud and clear, I did," allowed Mr. Ben. "What's it signify, son?"

Warren brightened a somewhat when Mr. Ben called him son, and so, I thought, did Callie.

"John, you estimated not quite two miles to that settlement," said Warren one more time. "We've heard what Eliphas Levi says about a straight walk of four thousand five hundred steps. How long is a step?"

"Different lengths for different folks," I replied, "but in the army, when they figure out stride scales, they call the average step thirty inches—two and a half feet."

"Two and a half feet," said Callie after me. She sat by the table, and she'd taken pencil and paper too. "Let me figure here."

She scribbled fast, a-sticking out her pink tongue.

"And two and a half feet is thirty inches," she said. Then she read out loud to us. "Forty-five hundred steps times thirty inches comes to one hundred thirty-five thousand inches."

Mr. Ben stroked his moustache. "That's a right many inches," he said.

"Divide by twelve," went on Callie, "and that makes eleven thousand two-hundred and fifty feet."

Warren took her paper and checked the writing on it. "Correct, Callie, your arithmetic is good," he said. "And eleven thousand two hundred and fifty feet is—let's see—in miles—"

"I'll figure that, too," said Callie, her pencil going like the wind. "A mile is five thousand two hundred and eighty feet. Two miles are ten thousand and five hundred sixty feet." She looked up at us, all round. "That's six hundred and ninety feet more than the forty-five hundred steps. An overage a little longer than the two-twenty stretch at a track meet."

"By God!" Mr. Ben hit his fist on the arm of his rocking chair. "Then that's how come them to want my land, so's they can make their straight track across my yard and on there beyond."

"On there beyond?" Warren repeated him.

"By God!" Mr. Ben said again, louder. "That would carry it onto the land of that sorry Sim Drogus. How'd you like to come with me, John, while I go have a little talk with Sim Drogus?"

"Wait a second," said Warren. "We've got more to say about this straight track of the Shonokins."

"What more's to say?" Mr. Ben wondered him, and Callie, too, looked at Warren with questioning blue eyes.

"I'm thinking about what's in other books of mine, books I wish I'd brought along," Warren said. "For instance, Francis Hitching's *Earth Magic*. Considerations of the ley lines of power, in England and a few in this country." He was as solemn as a preacher. "They spell it l-e-y, and that seems to be a word older in England than the Anglo-Saxon."

"Ley," Callie repeated him. "I've read books by Willy Ley, about all sorts of strange things."

"Willy Ley's name was German. But ley lines—they seem to have been brought to our attention by Alfred Watkins—are straight lines, straight as if drawn by surveyors. Like this one from the Immer Settlement to the edge of this place, not quite forty-five hundred steps."

"This is all plumb new to me," I said. "What's a ley line supposed to do for a fellow?"

"That's hard to say," Warren replied me. "All the discussions of them either want you to swallow all the wonderful theories—there's another interesting book by Colin and Janet Bord, they call it *Mysterious Britain*—that seems to think the ley lines can give power to ships from outer space. All sorts of other works sneer at these ideas, say that the lines are straight only by coincidence. But I'd say, that calls for lots and lots of coincidence."

"You're a-moving several laps ahead of me, my friend," said Mr. Ben.

"I just don't want to miss anything. I'll try to make it simple. Hitchings gathers all the evidences he can about a ley line as a power line. It runs straight, connecting points of mystic power. He maps one out in England that's more than three hundred miles long, and it runs through all sorts of mystic sites like the Cerne Abbas Giant—that's a big figure on a hillside—on through Stonehenge, and beyond to more and more, all the way to England's eastern coast." His eyes shone at us; he was excited. "What we have here isn't anything like that long a line, but it seems to touch some highly interesting things. That's including the rocking stone that John and I saw—and felt."

"I don't get no sense from it," said Mr. Ben. "Anyhow, I'm a-honing to go talk to Sim Drogus about what he's a-trying on with me."

"A straight line has power anywhere," said Warren. "A race course is fastest when it's straight instead of curved, like the two-twenty stretch Callie mentioned. You know it's true when you drive on a straight road, the sort they have out in Kansas. Before you know it, you're doing ninety, a hundred miles an hour, and here comes the state trooper to slow you down."

"That's true enough," put in Callie.

"Maybe it's what you showed us in your book," I added. "A forty-five hundred stepway could fix things so they could raise their dead."

"And a very good reason for them, too," went on Warren. "In any case, I judge the Shonokins want their power track to run on the proper distance right through your land, sir."

"If they got to have it forty-five hundred steps long, why in the name of all that's pure and holy don't they run it the other way from that there Immer Settlement they've done took over?" Mr. Ben more or less spit out.

"Because they want to use those points of power going this way," said Callie. "I can see that. The power must start right where they are—"

"You're right, my dear!" broke in Warren, not at all polite, but you should ought to have seen her light up when he called her that. "And what I showed John in Eliphas Levi gives us the clue that John pointed out. They're convinced that a long enough straight track might make them able to call up the dead, including that Shonokin who's lying on the way right now."

"Where he's a-laying, he holds them back," said Mr. Ben, hard as a flint stone. "John acts like he's sorry for that one, but me, I can't be. Jackson, all this you tell is right interesting. But I'm overdue to visit Sim Drogus. John, I asked you before, how'd you like to come along?"

"If you want me, Mr. Ben."

"Sure enough I want you. I might could be glad for a witness to whatever happens."

He got up from where he sat, slow and strong all through himself. His brows dragged themselves together in a frown I'd not have liked to mean me, and his moustache sort of frowned, too. He walked across the room and yanked open a drawer and took out a blue pistol. Callie watched him while he flipped out the cylinder and spun it to check the cartridges in it, then flipped the cylinder back and shoved the pistol down into the waistband of his suntan pants.

"Daddy," said Callie, in a voice you had to strain your ears for, "do you need a gun to talk to Mr. Drogus?"

"Not him, maybe, but I don't know what I'll meet outside my door," said Mr. Ben. "The way things have gone on today, a man can need something to shoot with, air minute and air step." He nodded to me. "Come on, John."

He was fierce about it, but, just as he'd said, things had gone on to make a man fierce. He tramped to his door and out of it and down in the yard. I went with him. Together we headed off the other way from the track, a-following that twisty road where Warren had driven us in the night before.

I had me some time to recollect some stuff I'd heard tell about other straight tracks in America—most of them up North, in places like Rhode Island, New Hampshire. Up where, from what I'd gathered from Warren's talk, the Shonokins had mostly been a-showing themselves. Power in tracks like them? It might could be that it was a late thing for the Shonokins to find it out. Maybe if they'd had such power all the way back yonder, they might could have used it to fight off the Indians in those long-ago wars. Maybe. Who knew? Who could know?

The trees looked all right on both sides of our way, not how they'd appeared on the way to Immer Settlement, when you'd swear they were a-lying in wait. "How far off is this man's place?" I inquired Mr. Ben.

"Oh, not as much as a quarter mile," he said back. "He's the only neighbor could have heard me shoot." He made a nasty noise in his throat, and spit on the ground as he walked. "John, if that Shonokin I hit is dead the way you say—well, I've allowed maybe I should ought to feel bad, but I don't. Brooke Altic told you the Shonokins ain't true men. To shoot him was more like to shoot a bear that raids a hog lot, or a fox that robs a henhouse."

"There may be a lot in what you say," I told him. I studied a thicket of balsam by the side of the twisty, rutted road. "This Sim Drogus man, does he live by himself? Is he single?"

"He sure enough is. I ain't nair heard tell of the woman who'd take up with such a sorry somebody, even if he does make money by a-lending it out at big interest. Well, maybe one woman that lives by the side of his place, that mean old maid Hazel Techeray. That'd be a double dose of meanness if they was to marry."

We made it round a curve of the road. "Yonder's where he roosts," Mr. Ben said.

A place was cleared off amongst the trees, with grass and red wild flowers on it. Back beyond, there rose a big face of rock, and in the rock was a fold hollowed out, just big enough for a cabin to be set into it. And that was no way as good or honest-looking a cabin as Mr. Ben had. It appeared like to be all patched together from gnarly old logs, with a warped plank roof to it. That roof had mossy green a-growing on it, and the cabin itself was crooked; it sure enough hadn't known the use of a plumb bob when it was built. The glass of the windows was broken and stuffed with rags.

A scrawny dog was in the yard and showed its teeth to us, but didn't bar us out as Mr. Ben led the way to the door.

Somebody opened that door and stuck half of himself out to blink at us.

"Yes," Mr. Ben grated his voice. "There you are, Sim Drogus."

Sim Drogus came out on his worn-down door log. He was just a scrawny little fellow, big only in the ears and the feet. You could have put your thumb and finger round his little cornstalk of a neck. On his face he had a week's growing of muddy-brown whiskers, and his nose hung down like a broken twig over his slobby mouth. His watery eyes were set so close together that he could near about have looked through a keyhole with both of them at one and the same time. He had on patched shoes and about two and a half dollars worth of old clothes that would have been better off in the washtub.

"Mr. Ben," he said in a whining voice, and made a shaky smile. "How you come on? Me, I ain't been so good of late. Kind of ailing."

"Which I'm sorry to hear that, Sim Drogus," said Mr. Ben, and he didn't sound sorry a bit. "Though you might just could wind up worse off air minute now."

"I do hope and pray not." Sim Drogus blinked his weepy eyes at me. "I ain't got in mind I know this here gentleman."

"My name's John," I said.

"John," Sim Drogus repeated my name. "John. Seems like to me I've heard tell of you in these parts, you and your silver-strung guitar."

"Sure enough," put in Mr. Ben, the grate still in his voice. "Likely you heard tell of him from somebody like that sorry Shonokin, Brooke Altic."

Sim Drogus swallowed. I saw his Adam's apple make a

shiver up and down again. But he didn't say a mumbling word to that.

"All right, the howdies is over and done with," said Mr. Ben. "Let's us get down to business, and I'll be plain about it."

"You're always plain and to the point, Mr. Ben," said Sim Drogus. "How come you come visiting today?"

"I'll tell you for how come," said Mr. Ben, very soft. "Are you the one that went a-running to them deputy sheriffs and told them there'd been shooting on my place?"

"Shooting?" said Sim Drogus, like an echo, and once again his Adam's apple went a-quivering up and down. "Deputy sheriffs, you say? Why, I ain't had no talk with no deputies, not this livelong day."

"Well, somebody did," Mr. Ben said back. "And you're the only one lives close enough in to hear to my place."

Sim Drogus blinked and swallowed, pure down scared to death. "Hazel Techeray was over here this morning from yonder where she lives." He pointed west, with a hand like a dried-out root. "Come to norrate to me about somebody other is a-having his place sold up by his creditors, and might could I be interested to go there, bid on a couple things. Could be I mentioned the sound of shots to her."

"To old Hazel Techeray." Mr. Ben spit out the name. "She should ought to be named Witch Hazel. She'd cross hell on a rotten foot log to make trouble for me, or air other honest man."

"Well, I nair told no deputy nothing, no way," said Sim Drogus.

"I see." Mr. Ben turned on his heel to go off. "If that's the whole thing you got to tell me," he said, "I won't use up no more of your valuable time, Sim Drogus. Only I'll tell you, I'll be right obliged to you if you wouldn't make no talk about my doings to old clatter-jaws like Hazel Techeray."

"Hold up a second," spoke up Sim Drogus. "Might could be I can put a little business in your way."

Mr. Ben swung back to face him. "What business you wish to do with me?"

Sim Drogus licked out his tongue to wet his loose lips. That tongue looked long and pale, like a lizard's. "I was a-thinking, if you had some of that real good blockade to sell—"

"If I had air such a thing," Mr. Ben cut him off, "and I ain't a-saying I do have, not for a second—if I did, I wouldn't be such a gone gump as to sell it to you. You drink too much the way it is, you'd be better off to take the pledge."

That was something meant to rile Sim Drogus, but he didn't dare rile. "Maybe I'd do right to take a pledge," he said.

"If I thought you'd offer to sell me this land of yours," Mr. Ben said, quieter, "we might could agree us on something there."

"No, nothing like that," said Sim Drogus. "Somebody else wants to buy it. Wants to pay a lavish price for it. A right nice fellow."

"Brooke Altic, maybe," I guessed.

"You know Brooke Altic, John?" Sim Drogus grinned at me, with brown, broken teeth. "He's got money. He wants more land. He'll pay well. And he'd do the like thing for Mr. Ben here."

"I wouldn't sell Brooke Altic enough of my land to dusty his shoes," said Mr. Ben, and tramped back to the road without another word. I followed along with him. Sim Drogus stood and watched us go.

"Did you hark at that, John?" Mr. Ben questioned me.

"Yes, I did. The Shonokins want his land."

"His land, over here the far side of mine. And that means they've purely got to have my land in between, to run their straight track through."

"I was a-thinking that," I said.

Mr. Ben blew out his breath through his moustache. "Well," he said, "let's us get on back home and find out what happens next, if the finding out can be found."

"Yes, sir," I agreed him, a-looking off the road amongst some junipers.

"What you see yonder, John?"

"Can't rightly say if I saw aught," I said.

Because I hadn't truly made it out, plain to my eye. A movement there in the thick of the green branches, a flash of blue color there. Not Sim Drogus, he didn't wear blue. Not a Shonokin, either, as I reckoned, unless maybe Brooke Altic in another suit of his sharp clothes. Anyway, I didn't think it would be Altic; no, nor yet Jackson Warren, come out to meet us halfway, the way he'd met me on the track to Immer Settlement.

"All right, then," said Mr. Ben, "let's head on home."

And on we went. He kept a-looking straight ahead, but I kept a-spying over my shoulder into the woods behind, a-spying into the woods, to make out if I could see whatever or whoever was there, one more time.

VII

We didn't make a great much of talk on our way back to Mr. Ben's place. Once he did growl out, "Forty-five hundred steps," and once again, "That low-flung Sim Drogus." I replied him not a word, but I kept on a-looking over my shoulder.

Sure enough, whoever or whatever had been back there in the hemlock was still a-staying with us, and not far behind either. Once it popped out a shadowy lump of a head from behind a bunch of laurel, and showed for just a scrap of a second, at the left side of the road. A moment later, closer in, I saw a sort of bright-bluish flick of cloth. So it wasn't Sim Drogus at least; his clothes didn't shine like that. In any case it didn't come all the way up on us, and I didn't make a mention of it.

Mr. Ben reached his porch and walked up the steps and in. Callie and Warren were a-sitting together at the table, a-snapping a crockful of early green beans. They acted plumb glad to see us back, and harked at what Mr. Ben had to say about the talk with Sim Drogus.

"That's informative enough, I'd say," said Warren. "For the Shonokins to run their straight line of power, they'd need not only this front yard but some of his land beyond, too. Maybe they want to extend it for miles, to pick up additional power for whatever they want to do."

"They talked money to him, and that's what he flaps them big long ears to hear talk about," growled Mr. Ben.

"I'll vow and be honest to tell you, this here would be a better part of the country if Sim Drogus just hung his old coat over his arm and took off for some other place."

"I feel sorry for him," said Callie, like the good-hearted soul she was.

"And so do I," said Warren, "particularly if he's getting involved with the Shonokins. But look at these beans we've made ready for noon dinner."

"It will be a little late if I cook them with a bit of bacon," said Callie.

"Then maybe there'll be time enough for me to take a walk in the woods," I said, and headed for the door.

"What you figure to find out there?" Mr. Ben inquired me.

"As to that, I can't rightly say," I replied him truthfully.

"Here, John," he said, a-reaching out his pistol to me. "Carry this here along with you."

"I do thank you, but I don't aim to shoot at aught," I said. "I'll be back in, say, maybe an hour."

"Dinner will be ready by then, John," called Callie from at the stove.

"And I'll eat my bait of it," I promised her, and went out.

At the front of the house, I went to the right corner and looked carefully to the back. The other way round would have taken me spang into the open, by the backyard and the buildings there. Where I was this side, I could slip into a little thicket of young pines grown up where some bigger ones had been cut down. So in I sneaked, careful not to shake a needle on a branch. On the far side I stooped low and made it into the shadows under a big, low-branched oak. There I harked and harked, and heard not a thing except a yellowhammer a-tapping somewhere to get him a worm. I spied out some more cover, and kept a-going my way in it, back to a place opposite that road to Sim Drogus's. I thought of whatever it was had made it a business to follow us along, and kept my eyes to the ground. A little movement ahead, a-taking advantage of air bush and air bunch of weeds on my way, with my eyes fixed on the ground. At last they spied out what I'd been a-hoping to find.

You couldn't rightly call it a real track. It was just a little damp scrape in some moss at the foot of a big old buckeye. But something had made that scrape, and not long before. Bent close to the ground, I spied here and there. Sure enough, a pebble had been kicked out of its bed, on the way into the woods from the road. That showed me I was on the right trail.

I still kept myself bent down so low I could have put my hands to the earth. I studied here and there and yonder for more signs of something a-going. I made out a little balded-off clearing in the trees ahead, and when I got to the edge of it I saw a real track in the dirt. It hadn't been made by Sim Drogus's old patched-up shoe; it looked to be made by a rubber sole, and not an awfully big one, either. Whoever had left it there wouldn't be too big to handle if I had to. But I didn't show myself in the clearing. I moved in the shelter of the trees all the way round, till I got to where I could see more traces the other side of the clearing. They led off in a way that would get up behind Mr. Ben's cabin.

Gentlemen, I made my moves right carefully along that line of marks. When you track something or somebody, don't get to thinking that because you don't see it, it can't maybe see you. I didn't move directly over the marks, but close enough at the side so I could make them out. I still used air clump of bushes, air tree trunk, to keep myself as much out of sight as I could. A-going along thataway, I may have traveled a hundred steps on the trail of what I hunted. Until I came to the edge of a little run of water, just a trickle through the woods. And on its soft clay bank was a sure-enough footprint.

It had been driven there by a shoe with a cleated sole, most likely what you call a tennis shoe. And there was water a-running into it; but it wasn't full up, nor yet near to. Whoever had made that track had made it right then. Was close in to me, right that selfsame moment.

I spied across the water. Another track showed there. To just follow flat on, I'd have to pop into the open. What if the somebody was a-watching back on his trail for me, with something in his hand beside an all-day sucker? I looked carefully up the little stream and then down. Bushes grew close below there, their twigs a-coming from both sides and in touch of one another. I slipped down to where those bushes were.

But I knew that if I went through them, the branches would wave to show me to air eye that might could watch from the other side, and the twigs would rustle loud enough to advertise me like a brass band. So I snaked on below the bushes, and slid round them and stepped over the run to the far side. On my hands and knees I crawled to where I could see the second track on the bank. I came so close to it, with my head so far down to the ground, I must have looked like a hunting dog a-trying to smell out what it was after. I looked Indian along the ground, almost at ground level. I could see some last year's fallen leaves that had been stirred up by a foot. I crawled to them, and saw that beyond them the trees pulled apart to make a little clearing. In the clearing I saw what I'd come out to track up on.

Right off, I knew it was a woman. She was down on her knees but not, as I figured, a-praying. A woman—and Jackson Warren had allowed that nobody had air seen a female Shonokin. At that, this was a regular human woman, with a big spill of shiny brown hair. She was dressed up in a bright blue blouse and a skirt made like a quilt, squares of all different colors, in a pattern that looked like what lady-folks call the Sawback Road. Where she knelt she'd pulled together a little pile of sticks, and as I watched she struck a match to set to it.

I straightened up and stepped into the clearing. "If I might could ask you, ma'am," I said, "how come you to make a fire on Mr. Ben Gray's land?"

She almost whooped, she caught up her breath so hard. She stood up, too, and goggled at me with her stretched-out, iron-colored eyes. Her wide mouth, painted as red as fresh blood, popped open.

"Who are you?" she sort of breathed at me.

"My name's John, and don't be scared, I'm not here to do you air hurt. What might could I call you?"

She didn't reply me that right off. She still looked at me, and I looked back at her. She was maybe somewhere in her forties, a-trying not to seem to be that many years. She was plump above and below her small waist. Her hair, you might could say, was the color of government whiskey that had been aged in the barrel, and her eyes, as I've said, were dark as iron, with specks of brighter green. On her feet were blue canvas shoes, and the blue of her blouse was what I've heard called peacock blue; though peacock feathers have eyes in them, all over them.

"You're a foreigner," she said, her voice all shaky. "I don't know you none from round here."

"No, ma'am, I'm just a visitor hereabouts. What name might could I call you?"

"Hazel Techeray," she said, and she smiled an impudent-faced smile, like as if that name should be good news to me.

I was a mite surprised to hear it, and that's a natural

fact. From what Mr. Ben had said about her, calling her Witch Hazel Techeray, I'd more or less reckoned she'd be some sort of ugly old woman with a cast in her eye, maybe a-riding on a broomstick. But Hazel Techeray had looks, though if a man had sense he'd feel put on his guard by such a look as she gave me out of that green-specked eye.

"And you call yourself John," she said, the slow way some women use when they're a-trying to be specially nice. "John, eh? I think you're the one who plays the silver-strung guitar, aren't you?"

"You seem to have been a-hearing a couple things about me," I said, and wondered myself if she hadn't maybe heard them from Brooke Altic.

"Yes," she said, and that little fire at her feet crackled as it began to rise up. "John, did air a woman tell you that you're a right fine-looking man?"

"Not many," I said, for not many women had air said such a thing to me, not unless they reckoned they'd get something out of me for the saying of it. "But I said, I wondered myself why you wanted to build that fire here, since it's a warm day and I didn't think you were a-fixing to do some cooking or the like of that."

"No, John. I just thought I'd make a wish."

Still she smiled on me. Her teeth were white and strong and more or less hungry-looking in that red mouth of hers. A wish, she'd said. I thought on how I'd heard tell of wishes made in certain ugly names, by folks who'd made them to do somebody harm.

"Just a little old simple wish," she said one time more. She reached into a pocket of her patchwork skirt and out came her hand with a pinch of purple-looking dust in the fingers. She flung it onto the fire, which sent up new flames that same shade of purple, with pale, greasy smoke.

"I made my wish before this," she said, with the words

spaced out like as if she was a-reading them out of a book. "I make it now. There was no day when I have not seen my wish fulfilled."

I'd heard those same words spoken before, long years back. They were what a witch person says to do you harm.

The purple fire cracked and popped as it grabbed the twigs. I had an ugly sense of a crowd gathered close round us—a crowd, maybe not of people, maybe not Shonokins even, but a crowd. Close in, close enough to see if I looked over my shoulder. I didn't look. I knew words I'd better say my own self, another set of words, and say them quick.

"Hazel Techeray," I said, a-remembering the thing as I repeated it over, "I forbid you this house and premises. I forbid you the sheds and stables. I forbid you each bed, that you may not breathe upon them. Breathe elsewhere, until you have climbed air hill, until you have counted air fence post, until you have crossed air water. And thus dear day may come again into this house, in the name of the three holy ones of power."

Right as I finished, the fire blinked out, like as if somebody had doused water on it. And that sense of the crowd all drawn up behind and round us, it went, too, and I well knew that she and I stood there alone.

"What's all that you said?" she sort of jerked out.

"Something I recollected pretty well from a book called *The Long Lost Friend*," I replied her, a-keeping my voice easy. "It's not a far off different from another thing I've heard said from another book called *Albertus Magnus*. And it backs a witch spell away from a place, away from people." I smiled. "Appears to be a-working right well here, doesn't it?"

She tried to give me a smile back, but her wide, red

mouth shook and twisted and her eyes couldn't look straight into mine.

"So you know witch stuff too, John," she said.

I shook my head no. "Only just enough of it to do something against it."

She reached out a hand to me. It was a slim one and a soft-looking one, with a ring on it, but I didn't take it.

"John," she said, "you're a witchman and I'm a witch-woman. We can help each other. If you're a stranger hereabouts, why not do yourself some good? You've got power—"

"At least enough to blink out your spell-fire for you, Miss Hazel. I don't guess it will do you aught of good to build another against Ben Gray and his place." I made a guess. "What will the Shonokins say if you go back and tell them you failed? What would Sim Drogus say, if you care about him?"

"Care about that skimpy little Sim Drogus?" Her voice climbed high and sharp. "Care about that little old scrap of nothing? John, you and I are more the right kind to care about one another."

"I don't want to hurt your feelings," I said, "but I'm not the right kind for you, not for a second."

"Wouldn't you want to be happy, John?" she almost squealed. "Don't you want money, want a big place in this world? You need money, I can tell that. I doubt if you have as much as four dollars in those old clothes of yours."

"No, ma'am," I agreed her. "Nowhere as much as that. Nor do I need it. I'm a kind of expert in a-doing without money."

I looked her up and down. Her pink face wadded itself up with anger. She dived her slim hand down into the front of her blue blouse. Out it came again with a long, lean knife, sharpened bright on both edges.

"We'll see," she gritted at me, and made a slash at me, a-trying to give me both edge and point at the same time.

Only, she nair gave me the one or the other. When I saw the knife flash out, I made a step clear of it. She struck so hard that when she missed she all but fell down. She scrabbled her feet back under her and turned. The knife came up again. I quick recited something else:

"I conjure you, knife, that would injure or harm me, by the priest of all prayers, who had gone into the holy temple of Jerusalem, and said: An edged sword shall pierce your soul that you may not injure me, who am a child of truth."

She'd fetched the knife high to make another stroke, but it fell out of her hand and went clank on the ground. She bent and tried to grab it up, and it slipped away from her. Again she reached for it, but I was there first. I kicked it out of her reach and got hold of it myself. I whirled it round my head and flung it far off amongst the pine trees.

"What I said against you then is likewise out of *The Long Lost Friend*," I told her. "Miss Hazel, you'd better try your witch ways on somebody else, because they won't work at all on me. Nor yet on Mr. Ben Gray, after what I spoke, nor yet on his property. Why don't you go home?"

"We'll see," she spit out again, and her pink face looked near about green. "We'll see."

"We've done already seen, and that's a fact," I said.

And I turned round and walked off from her, out of the clearing. And I knew she didn't make to follow.

I came along to the little stream and made a big step across it and headed back toward Mr. Ben's. Still I didn't look back to see was she a-following after me. Some of the strangeness had gone since I'd been in that clearing, but the woods still had an unchancy feel. I told myself that these were Mr. Ben's own woods, and most time must be good to be in, but not just now. Most of all, I felt I'd not want to be in them by night, when in the dark you hear dead voices talk and the trees are different from what they are by day, when they seem to move and reach for you with claws instead of branches.

I got to where I saw the house and the sheds and so on. No movement there. I walked round to the front door and in, and they all hailed me.

"Just in time to eat, John," said Callie. She was a-dishing up the green beans and bacon, with a plate of hot corn pone to go with them. Warren poured out some more coffee.

It looked too good a dinner to spoil by a-talking right off about what I'd been up to with Hazel Techeray. I ate with a true appetite. Not till we'd done and Callie and Warren gathered up the dishes did Mr. Ben ask me straight out what I'd seen and done. Then I gave them my tale.

They heard me out without them uttering a word, Callie with eyes big and round, Warren a-locking his brows to think, Mr. Ben with his hand a-going tap-tap-tap on the table next to his coffee cup. When I was done:

"What does it all mean?" Warren wanted to know. "What's this woman up to?"

"No good is what she's up to, and no good's what she's been up to in years," Mr. Ben said. "John, I do thank you for what you done for us out there."

"One thing's plain enough," I made offer. "At this stage, the Shonokins are a-fixing to get some things done for them by just ordinary human folks. Brooke Altic told me, they use men for some things, lawyers mostly."

"Sim Drogus ain't no lawyer," snorted Mr. Ben, "though he's sneaky enough for some kinds of polly-foxing lawyers. All I get out of him is, he'll sell land to the Shonokins, and I don't reckon he'll get asked to do that till they can get my land first. But a-catching Hazel Techeray up in their doings—what in hell's she to do for them, and why?"

"For profit, obviously," said Warren. "From what John says, she tried to put a spell on this place; only John took it right off again."

"They've flat got to use folks against us right now," I said. "They're not any much in a hasty way to come along at us past where that dead one lies in the ditch. Jackson here says that's one way of a-scaring them out. So they'll use ordinary folks that have joined their thing."

"I've always mistrusted Sim Drogus and Hazel Techeray," added on Callie, serving more beans to her daddy.

"And you had the right notion to mistrust them," he told her. "They're flat out the most mistrustable folks in all this part of the mountains."

"And," I said again, "since Brooke Altic and his Shonokins are held up by that dead one on their way here, they try to use our own kind against us."

Mr. Ben snorted. "Sim Drogus and Hazel Techeray ain't our kind," he said, and his moustache stood out on his face like a tom cat's. "And well Brooke Altic knows it."

"At least the Shonokins are checked just now," said Warren, his face thoughtful all the time. "I gather that if they want to use power, they must travel their track of power. Which, at present, they don't dare to do."

Mr. Ben flung down his fork. "Holy jumping Jerusalem!" he busted out, mad as a bear with ingrowing toenails. "Jerusalem, the golden name ever dear to me! Just what kind of a common, low-down, sorry sort of a creature is a Shonokin? They allow they ain't human, they act proud not to be human. And they ain't human, not when they don't dare face—"

"It's all right, Daddy," Callie tried to calm him down.

"It ain't all right, no such a thing!" he kept a-yammering. "Death? What kind of thing is it to fear death when you see it? Death is a part of life, folks, it's always a-happening; it'll happen to air living thing. Why!" He swung his flaming eyes from one of us to the other, all round the table, like as if he was a-picking us up for witnesses. "I've seen death, been close enough to death to hear the bells of hell go tingaling. In the war, why, death was a drug on the market. I've known what it was to stand knee-deep in death, men down dead all round me, some of them my choice friends. And I nair quit out, I stood up to death."

With that, he cut off his talk. He put his paper napkin out of his lap and got up and walked to the window.

"Is somebody out there, sir?" asked Warren.

"Who'd be out there?" Mr. Ben swung back to look at us again. "Won't be no Shonokins, that's for hellacious sure. And not Sim Drogus, he knows he don't dare step foot on land of mine. Nor neither Hazel Techeray; I reckon John's done slapped her out of her sneaky, snaky doings round here." He drew in his breath and smiled, but it was a sort of terrible smile. "No, folks, it's just us here, a-waiting for whatever they dream themselves up to do against us next time."

He tramped back and sat down. He picked up his napkin and fork again.

"All right," he said, "I got all that out of my system, and I reckon it done me a lavish of good. I thank you one and all for a-letting me blow off. Daughter, these here beans eat right good. They're as tasty a thing to eat as air I put in my mouth."

He dug in, and all of us dug in.

VIII

Mr. Ben had finished his dinner, and I reckoned he'd enjoyed it. He got up from the table and wiped his mouth on a paper napkin.

"I'm a-going out," he allowed to us. "There's one-two things to do on this here farm, and I've got to tend to them."

"Let me come with you," said Warren, but Mr. Ben shook his head.

"No, son, just me to go. The others of youins, stay inside here and keep an eye on things." He looked at me. "You specially, John."

Out he tramped. He looked right big just then; he looked ready for aught that might could come up. I went to the side window and watched him a-walking back to his sheds. I said to myself, yonder goes a somebody who knows pretty much what he'll be up to in case there's trouble.

The trees out there looked good, no creepy look to them like the ones I'd come on to in the woods off from the house when I'd met Hazel Techeray. These trunks looked like trunks, the leaves looked like just only leaves. They didn't bunch up into funny shapes. I had a hope that the words I'd said to Hazel Techeray had sure enough spoiled the curse she'd tried to put on there.

Warren and Callie had gone to the sink to do up the dishes. They acted happy to be a-washing and a-wiping dishes together. They laughed over something one or other

of them said. I had it in mind, this bad business was maybe
a-turning out good for the two of them, anyway. Callie
looked at Warren like as if he'd hung up the sun to shine,
and he was a-feeling good, too. He looked another sight
younger than he was always a-talking about. I didn't reckon
he was in much worry just then about how he was those
years older than Callie.

"Hello, the house?"

It wasn't air great much of a hail, that voice, that
woman's voice outside. It sounded more timid than
friendly. Callie put down her dishcloth and went to look
out the crack of the door.

"Dear heavens above, it's that Hazel Techeray," she
said. "Don't go out, John. I will."

"No, here comes your daddy," I said.

For, just as she spoke, Mr. Ben came a-walking back into
the front yard. He hunched up his shoulders, but he didn't
frown, he didn't smile. His face looked as calm and carved-
out as the face on a statue. I came and stood beside Callie
to watch, and Warren came up behind us.

Mr. Ben stopped on the path where Hazel Techeray
waited. If he looked calm, she sure enough didn't. She
made a sort of a gesture motion with her hands, like as if to
say she wanted to be friends, and she smiled at him.

"Yessum," said Mr. Ben, deep but not quite all mean.
"What can I do for you, Hazel Techeray?"

She blinked at him, and she fiddled her hands again.
"Mr. Ben," she said, "I come by here because I thought we
should ought to be good neighbors. It so happens I'm
plumb out of sugar at home."

She looked at him, a-hoping he believed her. She
squinched up her face. She looked embarrassed. Mr. Ben
stood and waited.

She tried again: "I thought I'd come by and ask, neighborly—can I maybe borrow half a cupful?"

She held out a shiny tin cup she had. Mr. Ben looked at it, then he looked at her. At last he shook his shaggy gray head.

"Hazel Techeray," he said, "you well know how come I can't be a-letting you have no sugar."

And well I knew, too. If a witch asks you for aught, and you give it to her, that can let her off from whatever spell you, or maybe a wise friend, has put on her. That's what's been a fact, in place after place I've been and seen things to happen.

"Now, Mr. Ben, that ain't got no neighborly sound to it," said Hazel Techeray, in half a whine.

"I'm sorry to have to agree you that, but it's up to me to look out for myself all the time, after you've been a-making out to try to witch me."

She let the hand with the cup drop to her side. She sort of bowed her head, the way things might have gone heavy on her.

"I'm sorry," Mr. Ben said, and he truly sounded sorry over it.

We harked and watched, from there inside the door.

"I mean," she tried again, "what I'd like to do is forget all old troubles there's been betwixt us." She shuffled her feet in their canvas shoes on the path. "Can't we maybe do that, Mr. Ben?"

He stood there, calm and cool as a judge on the bench. "You can best answer that question your own self," he told her.

"I didn't come over here to fight with you—" she started to say, and broke off.

"No, and neither do I want to fight with you," he said. "There ain't no power nor glory in a-fighting and a-whipping a woman. But no, Hazel Techeray, ma'am, I ain't got no sugar in the house I'd feel smart to give you."

He looked her up and down where she stood, and it made her to tremble herself, there on the path in her peacock-blue blouse and her patchwork-patterned skirt.

"And you can go tell that to the Shonokins," Mr. Ben added on.

"Shonokins?" she repeated him. "What would I tell to the Shonokins?"

"Just tell them you tried to trick me out of a cup of sugar, and I wouldn't trick out of it worth a cent."

As I watched and harked at him, I could tell he wasn't a-pleasuring himself when he talked to her so, but he knew what he had to do and say.

She turned herself round toward the road. She acted like as if she weighed about a ton to do it. Her head was down again, and her brown hair looked sort of tired.

"Oh," she said all of a sudden, the strongest she'd spoken yet. "That flower there, that there Indian pink—how pretty it is, Mr. Ben."

I could see the flower she meant, a-growing there in the yard. Some folks also call it a fire pink. It grew up on a little, slick green stem; it bloomed like a red star a couple of inches across. Hazel Techeray smiled down at it.

"How pretty it is," she repeated herself. "If you won't give me a little bit of sugar, Mr. Ben, couldn't I just have that there Indian pink to take home?"

Mr. Ben looked down at the flower, too. His face softened just a mite. He took a step at it, but he didn't bend down.

"If you sure enough want it," he said, and he sounded kind in the voice, "you'll have to pick it for your own self. I ain't a-going to exactly forbid it to you, but I ain't either a-going to give it to you. And, what I said before, you know just why I can't."

Hazel Techeray reached out her hand, but she didn't take that flower. Instead, she went a-walking off along the path to where the road was. When she got there, she turned herself back round.

"You and your friends here don't know what a fix you're in," she said, her voice a-making itself strong at last.

"We can make a right good guess," Mr. Ben called back to her.

He stood there where he was, with his feet set wide apart, and watched her as she headed off along the road toward where Sim Drogus lived, toward where she lived, too, as I reckoned. Then Mr. Ben turned and came up the steps into the house, where we'd all been a-harking at what went on. He looked heavy with his thoughts.

"You want to know a fact, John?" he said to me. "Somehow, I purely hated to do that to her just now. Refuse her thataway, I mean. I did hate it, even when I knew right well she was up to something against me."

"You did the right thing, Mr. Ben," I said. "The wise thing."

"Well, all right for that much," he said. "It's near about time for another little grain of blockade. I don't much drink a heap of it air one time, but I want a taste right now. To settle my stomach down, you can call it."

I looked past him into the front yard, at that pretty red flower Hazel Techeray had begged to him for. Then I turned back round. We all came and sat down while Mr. Ben poured.

"Leastways, she nair asked me for that there alexandrite I got in my pocket," said Mr. Ben above the rim of his glass.

"She was bound to know better than to ask for that," I

said. "Though for some reason the Shonokins want it, and want it with all their hearts."

"If a Shonokin has sure enough got a heart," he rumbled. "I'm a-beginning to wonder myself if these here Shonokins ain't just some kind of bad dream I'm a-having."

"The Shonokins are a reality indeed, Mr. Ben," said Warren. He'd got up with his drink and was a-stacking up dishes on their shelf. "They were a great and real danger up North, until my friend Thunstone checked them. Maybe they're still more or less a danger up there."

"And another danger here," said Mr. Ben, a-pulling his moustache. "A danger whatair place they come to. They're a-fixing to be a danger to me, and this here very morning they found out how I can be a danger to them."

Morning, I thought, this morning. Such a lot had happened since this morning. Now it was no more than two o'clock in the afternoon, to judge by the set of the sun outside.

I finished up my own drink. "Folks," I said to them all, "I reckon I'll just have me a lie-down and maybe a little nap. I didn't sleep so almighty much last night, you know."

"Go lie down on the bed in my room," Mr. Ben offered me, but I shook my head no.

"No, sir, my stuff's still out yonder on the porch. I'll unroll it and sleep there. I've mentioned to you all I sleep better outside. And, anyway, I can get the feel of the place while I sleep."

"Whatair pleases you," Mr. Ben granted me.

So I went out on the porch and flung my blanket over the quilt I'd used, and pillowed my head on my old soogin sack. I slid my hat down over my eyes to shut out the sunlight. I must have been asleep before one minute was gone.

In that sleep, I dreamed dreams. First off, as was right

usual, about my Evadare girl, how sweet she was, how sweet she made all heaven and earth. It seemed in my dream like as if she and I were out someplace a-picking blackberries. And then the dream changed on me. Now I thought it was a big outdoor meeting, and there was Brooke Altic, yonder on a platform, a-talking to a crowd of folks like at the singing. Now and then some fellows with long sticks, maybe they were Shonokins, poked here and there in the crowd to make the people cheer and hooraw for Altic.

A step sounded on the porch boards, and quick I sat up. It was Jackson Warren.

"You said, wake you up in a hour, John, and it's been about that." He looked at the watch on his wrist. "Three o'clock exactly. You certainly sleep lightly to wake up like that, all over."

"I do thank you, Jackson." Up I got, a-feeling good, rested, strong. I rolled my blanket and the quilt up and carried them and the soogin inside and stowed them in a corner where my guitar leaned.

"All right now, what's to be a-coming next?" Mr. Ben was a-wondering. "Appears to me like them Shonokins is sort of set back from us right this minute. Sim Drogus and Hazel Techeray might could be in their pay, a-working for them, but their work so far ain't turned out so good. Likewise, there's that there dead one of them John allows is a-laying on their track, a-scaring them off, a-keeping them sort of dammed away from us like a flood of water." He scowled over that, but it was a sort of happy scowl. "I don't know for certain but what I'd feel some better off if they'd just come and try on whatair they got to try on."

"It isn't apt to be any magic or sorcery, whatever they might try on," said Warren. "I gather that John was able to put an end to that particular sort of business on this property of yours."

"Oh, the hell," snorted Mr. Ben. "I've always heard tell that witchcraft couldn't work against a pure heart, only my heart ain't all the time pure. Sometimes I can be meaner than an old bear with a sore toe." He hiked up his brows at us. "Folks, I been bad in my time; just now, I could wish I'd been better as a young fellow. But the only thing I got in mind is, what if them Shonokins got them some kind of special witch stuff that our spells can't guard away from us?"

"I seriously doubt that they have that," I offered him. "Mr. Ben, witchcraft's an old thing. Most likely it goes back to the very beginnings of man, even the beginnings of Shonokins if they're older, all over this world. And the ways of whipping it are good all round. I'm not a-calling myself too easy, but at present I'd say we were way out in front of them on that line."

Somebody hollered the house from outside again. This time, it was a man's voice.

"I vow and declare, we're a-getting us a whole year's worth of company just this last two days," said Mr. Ben, and headed over to the door. He opened it wide and stood in it.

"Who's out yonder?" he yelled.

A-looking out past him, I saw three men there by the edge of the road. One was rangy, and the hair on his bare head was a big tawny shock. Another looked stocky and dark-skinned, with a sort of blue baseball cap on. He might could have had Indian blood in him. The other was smallish made, and he had a round face that seemed to snicker. They all of them wore rough farm clothes, but they looked to have shaved just that morning. Lots of mountain men don't shave once a day, some not once a week. These men meant company doings, I figured.

"Shoo, Mr. Ben, it's just us," said the rangy one. "You know us, all three of us. We just stopped by to tell you some news."

"Walk on out with me, John," said Mr. Ben, and he and I walked into the yard. The three men came along together on the path, close to the door.

"Fellows, this here is John, he's a visiting with me," Mr. Ben made the introductions. "John, shake hands with Lew Replogle."

The rangy one gave me his big, calloused hand.

"And this here is U. G. Bannion."

That meant the stocky one with the Indian look. "Howdy, friend," he said as we shook hands together.

"And likewise little Matty Groves," said Mr. Ben. "He's got him the same name as that there fellow in the old song, only he ain't been killed for a-courting another man's wife."

"Not yet I ain't," snickered little Matty Groves.

"I've had me some word of John," said Lew Replogle, who seemed like the one who was to do the talking for the whole bunch. "Matter of fact, last night at Brooke Altic's singing I heard him a-picking guitar and he give us that 'Murder Bull' ballad. John, I've heard a right much of good about you."

"Me, too, I have," said Matty Groves. "We've all of us heard tell good things about John, and I'm right proud to meet him."

They all grinned at me. Mr. Ben studied one, then another and another.

"And what's there I can do for youins?" he inquired them.

"Just only give us your idea on something," said Lew

Replogle. "We're all your neighbor folks, we always been a-getting on well with you, Mr. Ben. Weuns mostly reckon you for the foremost man of all this here neighborhood. So we naturally like to bide by your notions."

"Fact," U. G. Bannion seconded him.

"What notions would them be?" Mr. Ben inquired again. "I can't much speak to them without I know what youins mean."

"Well, now," said Replogle, "it's about a burying they want us to do for them."

"Whatair burying you a-talking about? Who is it wants youins to bury somebody?"

Replogle sort of hung back at that, and Bannion spoke up in his turn:

"Brooke Altic's done offered us a hundred dollars," he said.

"Brooke Altic?" Mr. Ben said the name like a cussword.

"All right now, Mr. Ben," tried Replogle one more time, "we know that him and you don't much agree on things together. But that there's your business, not ours. And he just offered us a hundred dollars in good money bills if we'd go up there on their track to Immer where one of their bunch is a-laying dead and gone. If we'd carry him to the old burying ground—the one where Brushy Fork Church used to be before they moved it to Aley's Crossing —and just put him in the ground there."

"And maybe we'd say a good word or two over the grave," put in Matty Groves.

Again Mr. Ben gave them a glittery look all round before he spoke. "All right, boys," he said at last. "If that's what it is, what's a-keeping you?"

Replogle slowly churned his big feet in their patched plow shoes. "It was a sort of funny proposition," he made out to say. "A hundred dollars—that ain't no kind of money for a fellow to turn down for just a couple hours of digging. But at first we wondered ourselves if it was the right thing. If maybe somebody shouldn't ought to go tell the law at the county seat."

Mr. Ben snorted so hard it fluffed his moustache. "If youins feel thataway, why not do that thing? There's been a couple deputy sheriffs a-using hereabouts today. They was right in this here yard this morning, to wonder had I been a-shooting at something or other. Youins might could track up on them and get their word on the matter and go by that."

"Aw now, Mr. Ben," Matty Groves sort of whimpered out, "we don't value them deputy sheriffs much. They nair come round about here to do aught of good to a hard-working man. We more-less thought we'd another sight rather inquire you what you felt about Brooke Altic's offer."

"It's an offer he made to you, not to me," said Mr. Ben. "How come you to run across him?"

"Matter of fact, it was him run across us," said Replogle. "We was all together on my place, over yonder." He pointed with his knuckly hand, off past the rear of Mr. Ben's property. "U.G. and Matty here had come to help me split up some shingles, and then here come Brooke Altic along and offered us that money."

"And being that John happens to be with us here," said Bannion, his eyes on me, "we'd be obliged to hear him for what thought he's got about it, too."

"The only thought I've got is, I'm a stranger guest here," I said. "I don't own the first thing hereabouts except these clothes I wear and the pack I tote when I'm along the way to go somewhere. I'm like you gentlemen—I'll wait to hear Mr. Ben speak on it."

"Yes, sir, and we'll all of us go by his word," promised Replogle; no doubt on earth but that he and those others set store by Mr. Ben. "Let him tell us to go ahead or stop, walk or stay on base. We know him and the Shonokins is at a fall-out with one another. We're neighbors to Mr. Ben and to the Shonokins, both of them. So we've come to him with it."

Mr. Ben wadded up his hard fists and clamped them down on his hard hips, with his elbows a-sticking out. I saw his face set itself into those strong, thinking lines it could take on.

"Why, hell's fire on the mountain, boys," he busted out at last. "Youins ain't got no need to get my yes or no in your own doings, so long as they're away off from this place I own. If youins feel like a-taking Brooke Altic's money, why go ahead—do what he wants."

"Bury that there dead Shonokin?" Replogle inquired him.

"If youins feel like a-doing it, and then there's that hundred dollars to divvy up amongst yourselves. Who in Tophet is Ben Gray to forbid you?"

They acted right glad to hear him speak up, like as if it was a word from a judge their way in a court of law. One after another, they said him their thanks and their good days, and off they went a-walking into the woods again. Mr. Ben kept his close-creased eyes on them till they were purely out of sight.

"John," he said, "did I tell them three men wrong?"

"I'm not about to answer that off the top of my head," I replied him, "but I feel you meant to tell them right."

"Glad to hear you say so. Let's come on back to the house."

Once we were inside again, he told that whole talk with the three men to Warren and Callie. Callie's eyes got bigger and rounder and scareder than ever, and Warren looked just a tad tight around the mouth.

"And now," Mr. Ben finished up, "the idee of them low-flung Shonokin skunks is, if their dead can be taken out of their way, they won't be none afraid to come here."

"And they're going to come here, Daddy," stammered out Callie. "As sure as we stand here, they'll come. Their way will be open. Jackson explained all that to us."

Mr. Ben flung out his thick arms. "Then let them come, I say!" he hollered in our faces. "I vow and swear, I've got tired of a-waiting on them here. That's how come I done told Lew Replogle and the others to go ahead with the burying!"

And I knew what he meant by that thing. It had been a-eating on him for hours.

"They brag they don't believe in no Devil?" Mr. Ben yammered. "All right, folks, they'll plumb believe in him before they get through with me. I'll give them the Devil— I'll give them hell with the lid off and the bottom of it a-shining right up into their faces!"

The way he sounded, you'd have reckoned he had it already done.

"I say sure enough, let them come here," he told us one more time, and he sounded calmer now. "Let them come with their meanness and try it on with me. I'm tired of just a-waiting round. I'll be here when they show up. They won't find this place of mine no joyful place to visit."

"By which," said Warren, "you mean that you'll be ready for their coming."

"That's the natural truth," Mr. Ben nodded to him. "Hark at me, son, my old grandsire come back from a-fighting in the Yankee war, to heir this piece of land from his daddy, and he built this here very house on it, with his own hands. He raised twelve youngins in it, and my daddy was the eleventh. And in time I heired it from him—my daddy."

"You feel it's yours," said Jackson.

"You can bet your neck I feel it's mine," said Mr. Ben, "spite of all them Godforsaken eternal Shonokins who ain't even got the final common sense to believe in the Devil. I swear to youins, one and all, if they come, I ain't a-going to be hard to find. I'll be right here on my ground, with blood in my eye and a chip on my shoulder. I want to get the thing settled with them. I'm a-getting dog-tired of all this here grief and trouble and hell raising they're a-trying to put on me."

He fell silent and waited for somebody else to say something.

"That was spoken like the brave, good man you are, Mr. Ben," I said, "and I'll be right here with you."

"And I," said his brave daughter, Callie.

"And I," said Jackson Warren, a-standing close to her. "Naturally."

IX

"All right, Mr. Ben," I said to him, and tried to keep my voice cheerful. "You've heard all of us say, we're in it with you to make a stand against them. And since you're in command—"

"Not me, I ain't in command, John," he chipped in on me. "I ain't a-going to be in command here, not by a long shot with a bush in the way. You're a-going to be."

I goggled when he said that thing, and I reckon that maybe so did the others. It was sure enough the last word on earth I'd expected from him.

"Looky here, John," said Mr. Ben, stubborn as a mule, air inch of him. "You purely got to be our captain in this here Shonokin business. And I call on Callie and Jackson to say likewise."

I shook my head at him. "Me?" I said. "Now, hold on. This is your place, and this is your part of the world. You know it like the palm of your hand. And I've not yet been hereabouts for more than about thirty hours."

"I'll tell you how come I said what I said," he came back. "It's because you know more than the whole rest of us about this kind of hellacious, spellbinding stuff, what them Shonokins want to try on here. John, just let me put it thisaway. You've been up against witch stuff and hant stuff and devil stuff before this, time and time again. And, what's more, you've whupped it—made it quit. By God, you're veteran against it. You're champion. So you'll be our captain and we'll be your troops."

"I agree with that," said Jackson Warren.

"But, Mr. Ben, you told me you'd been a sergeant once," I tried to argue him. "On my part, I nair in all my service got higher than PFC., nor yet wanted to."

"Oh," said Warren, "you could have made sergeant without half trying."

I recollected how, one time another they'd wanted to send me to noncom school, and how I'd always talked myself out of it. But I didn't say that.

"And I'll bet air man a dollar you've commanded men in your time," said Mr. Ben, still a-being stubborn.

"Well now," I had to admit, "there were times in the fighting when things got rugged in there. And other fellows sort of turned to me and wanted me to do the saying about what to do and what not to do."

"Naturally they'd be bound to turn to you," said Mr. Ben. "And that's what we're a-doing now. A-wanting you to say what to do."

"Exactly," Warren seconded him, and watched me as he spoke.

"Amen," said Callie, almost bright in her voice. "Amen."

"Well," I said again, "if you truly mean it, all right."

Mr. Ben grinned his teeth under his moustache. It was as harsh a grin as you could call for.

"Then it's settled, and we start to call you captain."

"No, you just call me John, and I'll call you all Callie and Mr. Ben and Jackson."

"Agreed," said Callie. "No formalities, but you tell us what to do. And right now, what is there for us to do?"

I knew right well that there'd be lots to be thought out

and told. "What's the time just now?" I inquired them, and looked out at the sun.

"It's just past three-thirty," said Warren, his eyes on the watch on his wrist.

"At this time of year," I figured, "the sunset will come round about six-thirty. We've got us a good three hours, as I make it. From now on, we keep here inside this cabin all we can. If somebody must go out, then only one at a time, with the rest on the alert."

"That there's a good order, John," said Mr. Ben, a-stroking his moustache.

"We'll close up all the windows, with boards or some such matter," I went on. "The last thing we do as the dark begins to come down, we'll likewise board up the doors. How many doors do you have in this house, Mr. Ben?"

"Just only the front and back, small a place as it is," replied Mr. Ben. "The front one here, and a back door in my room."

The front door was good and stout-made, as I'd noticed before that. "The windows to be all closed in, then," I said again. "If we have to do some shooting, we can aim out betwixt these logs where the chinking's been pulled out. Let's go have a look at the windows."

I headed into one of the bedrooms, then the other. Only one window to each of them, with glass in it. In Mr. Ben's room was the door he'd told of, the same, I recollected, he must have come in through to take his shot at that Shonokin. It was as good as the front door: it was made of stout planks with cleats crossways on them, and it had both a bolt and a lock. I turned the key and shot the bolt. Then Mr. Ben and I came out and climbed up the ladder to the loft where Jackson had slept the night before. Up there, they had just only a little small window, easy to make safe.

I stood and looked up at a trapdoor betwixt two rafter logs.

"That there goes up on the roof," Mr. Ben said. "What do you say; should we nail it shut?"

"There's no point in a-doing that," I decided. "We'll just make out to keep them from a-getting up on the roof. Our big job will be to watch all four sides down below."

"Sure enough," he said, "and there's four of us for the four sides, and all of us can handle guns. I'm glad I taught Callie how to aim and pull trigger."

We went down again. Jackson Warren was a-waiting. "What other orders, John?" he inquired me.

I'd been a-wondering myself about that very thing. This command had been shoved on me as sudden as the wink of an eye, and my mind was full of things for us to do.

"My judgment is that tonight is a-going to tell the whole tale," I said. "The tale both for us and for the Shonokins, and which one will come out top dog. After it's dark, I told you, we stay all nailed up in here, a-keeping watch all times. And no more than one of us to lie down while the others will stay on their feet and ready."

"Especially watchful by night," Warren quoted from the orders for an interior guard detail, the ones a soldier has to know by memory before they'll give him a pass to get out of the regimental area.

"That's got it," I agreed him. "And, after dark, no fire yonder on the hearth, even if it gets airish and chilly. We'll light one lamp but keep it turned way low, and stand it next to the door so as to throw no shadow on us to show through those spaces in the logs. And we've got to have some rations."

"That will be my assignment," spoke up Callie. "What rations, John?"

"A great big pot of strong, black coffee, naturally," I de-

cided. "Big enough to last the four of us all through the
night. And to eat, I'd speak for a kettle of soup we could
dip into whenever we felt we needed some."

She smiled about that. "I can do it. I've got things here
to make it. Chips of ham—good ham, Daddy's own smok-
ing—and some cut-up stew beef, and elbow macaroni, and
those green beans left over from dinner." She thought that
much over. "Yes, and about twelve different seasonings,
and some canned tomatoes."

"That sounds right good, Callie," allowed Mr. Ben.

"Second the endorsing motion," added in Warren. "Callie, let me help you."

They started right in a-fixing the ham and beef in a kettle, as cheerful as two folks a-getting ready for a picnic. Mr.
Ben looked over all the guns he'd laid out for us. He'd put
out ammo, too, handfuls of different-sized cartridges, on
the edge of the table. I studied those handfuls. Too bad we
didn't all have guns the same caliber, but that couldn't be
helped just then.

"Me," said Mr. Ben, "I'm a-going out to the shed for
some boards to close up them windows and all like that.
You got us figured safe so long as it's daylight, John, so I'll
go. And likewise I'll tend to things one more time so's
they'll not be no reason to go out at night. Thank the good
Lord I ain't got no animals on this here place to worry
over."

Out he went. I drifted to a window to watch.

Again I said to myself, the trees all round the cabin
looked good, looked trustworthy to me. I figured my quick-
said spell against Hazel Techeray must have done its work.
At last things could be natural in that yard and for maybe
a good space round it. I hoped so, anyway.

I studied over what orders I'd given out for whatever
trouble might could come, and decided that I'd just let it

be enough said right then. A man could talk too much, without a good reason to do it. If there'd be aught else to say and do, that could come up when the real business came up.

As she put things into the soup kettle, Callie started in to sing. It was a song I'd nair yet in all my life heard, to a strange, lonesome tune:

> "The silver is white, red is the gold,
> The robes they lie, they lie in fold;
> The bailey beareth the lull away,
> The lily, the rose, the rose I lay,
> Through the glass window shines the sun—
> How could I love, and I so young?"

Warren almost dropped a big iron spoon he was a-stirring the kettle with. "Callie, that's the most beautiful thing I've heard in years," he said, his breath all caught up to say it.

"You like it?" she inquired him, a-smiling. Sure enough, she'd sung that song just for him to hear.

"I've read it," said Warren, with his breath still caught. "It's in *The Oxford Book of English Verse*, and in some other collections. I've read it, I say, but I never heard the music. Where did you ever learn that?"

"My mother used to sing it when she was still alive. I imagine she got it from her old folks. They were all musical in her family."

"Beautiful," said Warren again, like somebody in a church house.

"Beautiful's the true plain word," I said, and went to pick up my guitar and turn a peg or two to tune it. "Go through with it again, Callie, and let me see if I can follow you along."

And, happy as a bird, she sang it over again, and I

backed her on the guitar. The scale was another of those old-timey modal ones I'd been told about, minor-sounding but not sure enough a minor, not really. And the song was as beautiful to hear as Warren had sworn.

On the last notes Callie sang, Mr. Ben slogged in, a-hugging in both his arms a big heap of planks of different sizes. He leaned them to the wall.

"Sure enough pretty-sounding, that there song," he sort of grumbled out, "but I don't know just how it'll help us out in what we got to do hereabouts."

"I can't agree you all the way on that, Mr. Ben," I said, a-putting my guitar back on my heap of gear in the corner. "I've heard it said, you can't have an army without music."

"Hah!" he grumbled out again. "All right now, whoever said such a thing as that, I want to hear tell."

"I believe that that observation is generally attributed to Robert E. Lee," said Warren as he watched Callie pour a glass jarful of home-canned tomatoes into the soup kettle.

"Oh?" said Mr. Ben, quieter this time. "Oh, him. That's all right then. Only I sure enough could wish that Robert E. Lee was right here with us in this here old cabin, to maybe help us figure out what to do against them torn-down Shonokins."

I could have near about wished the same thing; or, if we couldn't have some big, smart old general like Lee or Washington or Napoleon, I could have just wished for a few smart-thinking, sharp-shooting friends I knew. If Obray Ramsey could have been there then, as good with a deer rifle as he is with a banjo, which means first class. Or either Eddy Herron from up in the Toe River country, with his two tall sons Clay and Gavin.

"Mr. Ben," I said, "let's you and me get those boards you brought in up over these windows, against what might could try to come through at us."

I looked over the boards he'd fetched. There were some rough-sawed planks, and others that were just thick, split slabs of different trees. Mr. Ben searched out a couple of hammers and a handful of big spike nails, more or less the sort of thing that Jael the wife of Heber must have knocked straight through the skull of Sisera in the Bible—a common sort of trick, as I'd always reckoned. He and I went into the back bedrooms, first one and then the other, and spiked on planks over the windows there, from top to bottom. There was a bureau in each room, and we shoved the bureaus against the planks. Next, in the front room, we closed in all the windows the same way, with just cracks betwixt the planks so we could peek out from inside. It made the room sort of darkish, but light soaked in through the spaces where the chinking was out of the logs. Finally, we headed once more up to the loft, and just one plank was enough to block the little window there.

"How about that trap?" asked Mr. Ben again, with his eye on it.

"No, forget it," I judged. "We just might could want to get up there our own selves."

Down we climbed again. Another thought had started to feel itself round in my mind, a something I'd heard tell years before from an Indian chief I'd met at a county fair.

He was a leather worker, of the Osage tribe that has a reservation in Oklahoma. He'd been to government schools and was up to what the books allowed about this and that, but he likewise remembered the tales of his old folks; especially about the big wars that the Osages had fought with the Utes before the white man's government came along and put a stop to them. And he'd narrated to me what the old Osage war-makers believed, like this:

A part of the Osage religion was belief in life after death. They allowed that, if you should kill a man, his ghost would hang round. Then, the next time you had a fight, that ghost would come in on the side of the man you fought. By the time you killed three-four enemies, their ghosts would all pitch in to help whoever you fought next. And the odds got bigger and bigger, the more people you killed. The Indian who told me that was civilized, as I've said, but I got the notion he believed in what he was a-talking about. And now, when I recollected it, I wondered myself if there might not be some truth to it.

Killing? There come times when a man naturally has it to do. I didn't think much about things I'd had to do in war—I always try to forget that war as much as possible. But there were other things in my past.

For instance, there'd been Mr. Onselm, who'd fallen down stone dead when I struck dead the Ugly Bird that was his familiar spirit. And then Mr. Loden, a witchman who'd lived the most part of three hundred years before I'd used a charm of silver against him, silver that was destruction to his sort. And Hoph, who'd needed a silver bullet to settle his low-flung hash. And Shull Cobart, maybe the most devilish evildoer I'd air known in all my life; I'd fed him right smack into the skeleton hands of Kalu, the bone-demon who haunted Hosea's Hollow. Yes, and others. Not all of these had I struck down in battle, but I'd been the death of them as sure as if I'd gone after them with a double-bitted ax. Whenever I'd come to stand before the judgment seat, their blood would be on my hands, for good or evil.

It was enough to make me feel long in the face when I thought of fighting Brooke Altic. Only—hadn't Brooke Altic probably caused some deaths on his own part? Might not those ghosts come and work against him when the other ghosts worked against me—might they sort of cancel things out a little on my side? I couldn't know. I could only hope that.

Mr. Ben stowed away the hammers and nails and came to look into the soup kettle. "Now, that'll eat good some time tonight," he vowed. "And I feel that we're likely as ready for trouble as we can get. What do you say, John?"

"I say more or less the same," I told him. "How about you, Jackson?"

But he wasn't a-harking at me right that moment, because Callie was a-talking to him, and he hadn't an ear for a word from all the world else.

"I keep feeling so guilty," she said to him softly. "Why have I put you into all this, Jackson? What have I got you into?"

"You've got me into where you happen to be at the moment," he replied her, with all the meaning he could put into it. "And, come what may, I'd be glad to be beside you under any circumstances, Callie."

Mr. Ben watched them. His strong face-lines looked a heap gentler as he harked at what they said.

"I'm glad to be with you too, Jackson," Callie almost whispered. "You're strong and wise and brave. And we both trust in John."

"That's right," said Warren. "With John on our side, we really outnumber those Shonokins."

I stood and hoped to heaven that there might could be something in what they said. At last Warren looked round.

"Did you ask me something, John?"

"Nothing to matter," I said. "I figure I can count on you, against the Shonokins or the Devil they say they don't believe in."

"The Devil," he repeated after me. "That reminds me of what Sir Walter Raleigh wrote once, about the fallacy of frightening the Devil away."

"The Devil's supposed to be afraid of music," said Callie.

"Raleigh thought that charms and spells against Satan didn't make much logical sense," Warren went on. "He pointed out that a magic line drawn to pen Satan in wouldn't really stop a mouse. He reminded us that Satan hadn't been afraid to mobilize an army of fiends and make war on God himself."

"I heard tell about that at a camp meeting one time," I said. "The preacher allowed that once there was such a war, and Satan's side didn't last but three seconds against God's angels."

"I could wish we had a few angels with us, then," said Mr. Ben.

I put on my hat. "Folks," I said, "I'm a-going out for a while."

They all swung round on me and scowled their faces and stared. I'd nair before seen six eyes bugged out thataway.

"Hold on," said Mr. Ben. "You ain't a-going to do no such a thing."

"Hold on yourself," I said back to him. "You all chose me to be the captain here, and the captain gives the orders. All right, in a battle we need reconnaissance, we need information. I aim to scout out along that track of theirs—"

"How'll you dare do that, you gone gump?" Mr. Ben broke in on me.

"It's been a good hour since those neighbor-folks of yours came here to talk about a-fetching off that dead Shonokin to their burying ground," I made a reminder. "I want to be certain sure they did that thing. Likewise I expect to find out a couple other useful things."

"I don't like it, John," Mr. Ben argued at me.

"Sorry, but here I go," I said again. "Mr. Ben, you be in charge till I get back."

"What if you don't get back?" Warren inquired me.

"I'll get back, all right."

And, as I said that, I somehow knew I spoke the naked truth.

X

There next to the steps, I saw for the first time, leaned an ash stick, about three feet long and as thick as a hoe handle. I picked that up to carry along with me. And I stopped for a second to look down at the Indian pink that Hazel Techeray had begged for and hadn't been given. A purely pretty flower, that was, healthier to look at than the flowers round the Shonokin houses at Immer Settlement. As I studied it, I heard the *clickety-clickety* note of a seedeater. There it sat, black and white and little, in a beech tree. I headed on, but I didn't step onto that trail with its tingle. I kept to the woods beside it.

And, right off, they were another sight different woods than the trusty woods at Mr. Ben Gray's place. They had the feel I'd known in that clearing where Hazel Techeray had said her spell and made her witch fire, the feel I'd made go away with my own spell.

It was like as if the trees had a sort of life to them, like as if their trunks stirred like bodies and their branches moved like arms. Amongst their bunches of green leaves, you could make out something like faces, and not good-looking faces either. There'd be a shadowy green clump, with dark splotches in it like eyes, maybe like a toothy mouth, like a skull, sort of, or the face of an animal of a sort you weren't purely sure of. Well, that would mean I was out of the Ben Gray land and the spell I'd said to protect it. Here, there wasn't air good spell, and I doubted if it would much help to say one for whoever's land it was.

I said to myself that it was just imagination. I hoped that was so. I kept a-going along through thickets of unchancy trees. All the time I kept in sight of that Shonokin track, but I stayed off it.

Once again I called back to mind all those witch people I'd met with and some of them I'd destroyed. Mr. Onselm, Mr. Tewk, Shull Cobart; yes, and Mr. Howsen who'd served the wants of what they called One Other beside the Bottomless Pool on Hark Mountain. Likewise there'd been Polly Wilse, the witchwoman who'd stayed seventy-five long years in the desrick on Yandro, with all round her such things as the Bammat, the Flat, the Behinder. Shoo, the Behinder. I wished to my soul I'd nair had a glimpse of that, to give me the shivers from time to time all the years since.

As to these woods I walked, I'd come to reckon they must belong to the Shonokins, by those law titles they'd managed to get somehow or other. It stood to reason that they must own the land right up to Mr. Ben's yard, which now they wanted so that they could run their power track across it and on. Well, that made these same woods haunted, and that was a naked fact. I looked at a thicket. I had a notion of something on the move the other side of it. I even thought I heard feet, slow and heavy, a-keeping pace with me.

I stopped dead. If there'd been feet a-sounding, they stopped dead, too. Did whatever it was have an eye on me there? I strained my eyes, but I couldn't see aught through the branches. I only felt something, all the same. A something outdoingly big and sneaky.

I recollected what I'd been told about things they called dinosaurs, once thick and ugly all through this country. All gone now, all dead and gone. But then, you'd expect the Shonokins to be dead and gone, too, and they weren't. Nothing has to be dead and gone just because you don't know it's there. I hated the thought. I walked on. Imagination . . .

No birds sang in those woods. Then came the throaty rattle of a raven, off to my left. A raven a-talking on your left means, look out, you're in trouble. I'd another sight rather have had it on my right.

Just then, something did sure enough come into view, and my heart hopped right up against the back of my tongue.

It wasn't aught of a great big thing, at that. It scuttled in some juniper scrub, a quick flutter of something black. Next moment, it came out in plain sight of me.

A little black dog? No, and not a cat either. It might could have been a groundhog or a big weasel thing. No, not them. It headed for open ground amongst the trees ahead of me, and stopped there and slewed itself round to look at me.

It had big eyes that shone, pale and ugly, and it had teeth bare in its mouth, pale and ugly too. Those eyes and teeth shone like chips of feldspar. I pointed at it with my ash stick, and it went a-sliding away again, up there ahead of me. It sort of scrabbled its feet and headed straight across, like as if to draw a line over my path. I walked toward it, but at the line something made me stop and stand still. The little animal, whatever it might could be, went a-racing all the way round behind me and up in front again, a-drawing a circle round me. It crouched.

All right then, a spell was a-being put on me, a ring drawn to shut me inside. I recollected what Jackson Warren had said about Sir Walter Raleigh, how such a line shouldn't ought to stop a mouse. But I decided to do something other than just step over, another remembry from *The Long Lost Friend.*

I hiked up my stick in my hand and recited the words:

"Like unto the blessed cup and the wine, given unto the holy saints," I said, a-spacing the words out slow, "may I be guarded and defended in the daytime and at night, that no serpent bite me, no wild beast tear me, no weapons, no steel, no iron hurt me, no false tongue injure me, no rogue enrage me, and that no fiends, no witchcraft, no enchantment harm me." I raised my voice. "Amen!" I said, loud and clear.

Whatever that little black thing was, it was gone. I wondered myself however it could move so fast to get itself out of sight. I stepped on out of the circle it had drawn to pen me in and went a-walking ahead.

And there yonder, beyond the next belt of trees, there she was.

Hazel Techeray stood bowed over and scared-looking, like some naughty child that waited for somebody to beat on it. Even her clothes—the blue blouse and the quiltwork skirt—looked dull and timid. Her brown hair was swept down over her face. She stood and didn't look up at me.

"John," she said mournfully. "John. Your power's too much."

"And your power's too little, Miss Hazel," I said, and stopped next to her and leant on my ash stick and waited.

"My power?" she repeated me. "It's nothing, John. Not now. It's gone from me."

What new trick might could she be up to? But those words I'd said to her, before in the clearing and just now, when her little pet creature, her familiar if you'd care to call it that, had put away something from against me. The woods moved and sighed round us, but I didn't let myself feel scared.

"What's gone with your little familiar animal?" I inquired her.

"It—it's deserted me."

Her face was pale, right to her mouth that was red no more, just pale, sick pink. I felt a mite sorry for her.

"You tried another spell, and it wouldn't work," I said.

She twisted her face. "I only wanted to stop you. I had to see you."

"All right," I said, "you see me. How do I look?"

Another twist of her face. "Please listen to me, John. Have pity on me. I—I want to change sides."

That put me in mind of Brooke Altic's talk to me that morning, about winning sides and wrong and right sides. "Which side do you want to change to?" I asked of Hazel Techeray. "Which have you been on so far?"

She flung out her arms wide, and her hands trembled. She looked at me at last, with the unhappiest eyes on this earth.

"I was on the Shonokin side. I took orders from Brooke Altic, but that's no good for me now," she stammered. "John, I want to come and be with you and your friends."

And she swayed so that for a second I thought she might fall down there. I started to put out a hand to help her, but she got hold of herself.

"All this talk's because you think my power's the greatest," I guessed. "You just want to be on the side that's got the heaviest artillery."

"No. No, not that alone. It's—it's what they want me to do for them." She looked up, and her mouth twiddled, like as if she had had a stab of pain. "When I talked to Brooke Altic a little while back, he said—"

She stopped and shuddered.

"Said what?"

"I reckon he thought it was a reward of some kind. John,

you know the Shonokins don't have women amongst them."

"So I've heard tell, Miss Hazel. That makes it right peculiar that there can be Shonokins, just male Shonokins."

"Oh," she whispered out. "They use women—human women."

It was my turn to stare. "You don't say so."

"But it's true. And Brooke Altic wants me to come in with them, to—"

"I understand," I said, to keep her from a-saying words that might could bust her up. "Well, this explains things a little bit. But if Shonokins have human mothers, then they aren't pure-bred Shonokins, are they?"

She didn't bother to go into that. "And they want Mr. Ben Gray's daughter, Callie," she whimpered. "For the same thing."

"Her?" I said. "They'd better not hold their breath till Mr. Ben lets them have her."

Again she quivered her hands. "John, that's the real reason they want that jewel that means such a heap to him. They figure it for special with him. If they could get it, it would give them power to rule over him—make him do whatair thing they'd tell him. Even make him give Callie over to them."

Again I thought over my talk with Altic, how he'd wanted to trade me for my belt that Evadare had given me. He might could have noticed that it meant a right much to me. I'd heard of witch doings like that, with a lock of somebody's hair or a handkerchief, all like that. You could use such things to make a girl love you, they allowed, or cause a man to drop dead in the full of his health, or give you all his money. The Shonokins, who were a-knowing so much, would know about that sort of business.

"And now I want to get away from them," she said. "John, it's awful."

I studied over what she'd been a-telling me, digested it, you might could say. And I studied her over, too. She was scared to her soul; that was as plain as mud. For once, she might could be a-telling the truth of things.

"From what you say," I came out with, "you figure that our side's the winning side."

"Yes, because it's pure down got to be the winning side. Their side's the dark one—I don't wonder myself they don't much show themselves by the light of the sun." One more time, she made a sort of lost motion with her hands. "I confess I was a witch, John. I done all the mean things you do to get to be a witch. But—oh!" Her voice got loud and shrill. "I give it all up now; I see that the wrong way is the way down to hell, to hell!"

"Not so loud, Miss Hazel, we don't know who might could be hidden out to hark at us. I won't quarrel with you about the way to hell. But the Shonokins don't believe in hell. Maybe they're scared to."

"John," she almost wept, "I want to come along with you."

"If you want out of the mess you've put yourself into," I said, "your best move is to go home, wherever that is, and find some better business to follow than witchcraft."

I thought she was a-going to bust out crying, and I walked on away from her. I cut the heads off some weeds with my stick. I didn't look back at her, but I knew she stood where I'd left her, stood there scared to move or think.

Then a bird twittered somewhere, not loud, but a bird was there. The first, except for the raven, I'd heard since I'd left Mr. Ben's cabin.

I could see through the sneaky trees to where the Shonokin track was. I walked along, a-keeping in sight of it. I knew how dead straight it ran, how hard it was bottomed. I'd walked on it that day. And I knew how, if you were on it, you tingled. That was the power the Shonokins knew how to pick up with it, the power they planned to use against people.

And how would they fix to use it? They'd been sneaky all their thousands and thousands of years. They hadn't been able to stand up against the Indians when there'd been that fight with them. Oh, but then, probably, they didn't yet know how to get power by the drawing of those straight tracks. Where would the Indians have been if the Shonokins had known that? Now that they did know it, they'd use it. Their old enemies, those Indians, might not count for much with them these days. But there were people for them to use it against, bring down in conquest.

Some place in the Bible, the book of Joel as I seem to recollect, there's something about a sneaky attack. In those woods I said it over to myself:

A great people and a strong; there hath not been ever the like, neither shall be any more after it, even to the years of many generations. . . .

Could that maybe mean the Shonokins? There'd been the like of Shonokins all the centuries. Only, nobody had known they were there, getting smart as hell, getting strong, getting ready to strike. There was another verse about them:

They shall run to and fro in the city; they shall run upon the wall, they shall climb upon the houses; they shall enter in at the windows like a thief. . . .

But we'd closed in the windows with those big stout planks, and if a Shonokin should come a-thieving in, we'd be ready to disgust him with the job.

Now, I felt a touch of the stir in me that the track would

have given if I'd been on it. Just a whisper in me, you might could say. I looked over thataway.

Through a stand of little pine saplings, I made the thing out, that balanced stone. A breeze came up with a strong puff, and it swayed where it was balanced. Whatever it had in it, I could feel it, even off the track the way I was right then. I figured it must give some sort of strength to the track, or maybe the track's strength was stored up in it. Jackson Warren might could have said; I couldn't. I just only wanted to get on past it.

So on past it I went, and the feeling died out of me again. I was a-coming to where the dead Shonokin had been left in the ditch.

Another few moments and I could see the place. I saw that there were live things there, too. They were men, the same three that had come to talk to Mr. Ben. I made out that tall, knuckly Lew Replogle first. The others were little Matty Groves and the Indian-looking U. G. Bannion. They all stood on the far side of the track, and they looked down at what was there, and I didn't need a spyglass to know what it was.

The three of them talked a few words to one another. Then Replogle reached down and dragged something over close to them. It was like a sling or a stretcher, made of two long, rough-cut poles. I couldn't be sure, but I thought they were two oak saplings. I worked my way closer, all the time keeping under cover, and I saw how that stretcher was made. They'd put shorter pieces across and fastened them with cord or wire. And on the thing they now draped a ragged old quilt. I could make out that the pattern was Irish Chain.

Careful in all they did, they set the stretcher down, and then all of them stooped over and hiked up what was to go on it. The dead Shonokin, in his dark coat, his tumbled hair. He still hung limp, though he'd been dead for maybe eight hours—perhaps the Shonokins didn't stiffen up like people, like animals. They pulled him out straight on their stretcher and laid his hands on his chest, one crossed over the other. Then Matty Groves picked up another old quilt —Jacob's Ladder pattern, this time—and covered him up with it, over his head and all.

I thought they were ready to tote him off then, but Bannion was away amongst some trees. I stared to see what he brought back. It was flowers. He had a few azaleas, and some pink moccasin flowers in a bunch. He laid them carefully down on the quilt, just where the dead hands would be crossed underneath. Then he and Replogle picked up the stretcher and crossed the track with it, with Matty Groves a-following behind. I could see Matty Groves kind of skip, and figured the power in the track had jangled him.

They came into the woods on my side, and I hunkered low in some scrub so as not to be seen. I watched them head away with their burden. I felt good toward Bannion, because of those flowers he'd found to put on the body. They might could be more or less trifling men, if I was to credit what Mr. Ben said of them, but they had hearts. Human hearts.

I stayed hidden till they'd had minutes to get out of sight all the way. Then I moved carefully to the edge of the track, stooped down behind a pine tree, and sighted along it in the direction of Immer.

Shapes stood up on the track, along there. Shonokins, who'd come to see that their dead had been carted away, that the track was open for them to come to Mr. Ben's cabin door.

XI

Quick and quiet as I could make it, I slid back into the thick woods and hoped to heaven they hadn't glimpsed me. Now to make it back to the cabin again, report on what I'd seen. I headed back along the way I'd taken, with the strong sense on me of uneasy sorts of things amongst those trees and thickets. Overhead there slid a big old buzzard, likely on the look for whatair he might could devour.

These would be Shonokin woods, sure enough, bought by them some time or other. Not that I figured on them to be a-using round so quick after the dead one had been wagged out away from where he'd lain. But, I told myself, better to keep an eye and an ear cocked for whatsoever might could sneak up.

Because the Shonokins had their way clear to the cabin now, though likely they'd wait for dark to fall. When they'd been there before, during daylight, one of them had stopped a bullet right where he lived. And they couldn't stand that, not with all their knowledge and power and strength.

I came along opposite that place where the balanced stone gave its special nervish tingle. Their strength, I thought to myself again. They'd try to use their strength against where our weakness was, the weakness of men.

Oh, and they knew right well what was weak in mankind. Man is cruel, man is selfish. A hundred dollars, just a hundred dollars, had bought the services of Replogle and

Bannion and little Matty Groves to act as gravediggers for the Shonokins. The Shonokins had bought Sim Drogus, likely so cheap that they thought they'd stolen him. Had bought Hazel Techeray, then seemed to scare her out, but maybe she could be bought still if they could use her.

None of those were great strong folks, but then likely the Shonokins didn't reckon they needed strong folks. Likely they reckoned to take care of us with just a little small bit of help from some of the ratty sort.

Man's sure enough a selfish thing, a greedy thing. You ask just about air man what he'd wish for if he had just the one wish, likely he'd wish right off for a million dollars; wish that, even if he already had a million. And what kind of sorry wish is that? I skirted round a bunch of scrubby willows under some pines and gave a thought to what I'd wish for. Maybe the best wish would be for cruelty and selfishness to go off away from all the people on this earth. But all I could do was take it out in a-wishing, and try to do my own possible best to keep from a-being selfish and cruel myself.

That was the kind of thoughts I had as I went on toward a big mess of laurel, and all of a sudden quick I knew that something was a-hiding in yonder.

I upped my stout chunk of ash, ready. "Come on out of that!" I said, as sharp and mean as I could make myself sound.

It was Hazel Techeray who came out.

Right off I could plainly see, she was in near about the last stage of a-being scared. Her face, that had been rosy that morning, looked as white as a pan of milk. Even her wide, full mouth wasn't red anymore; it was a pale pink, like a tomato not yet ripe. She held out her hands to me, and they shook like two socks on a line in the high wind.

"Help me, John," she begged to me. "Oh, please!"

"I'd thought you were a-going home," I said.

"But I don't dare do that," she said. "I'm away off such a track. They'd come get me there."

And, gentlemen, she was sure enough in a state. Her body, that I'd seen so proud and sassy when we talked over back of Mr. Ben's house, a-filling out its clothes, now it looked all shrunked up inside them, like as if she'd lost pounds of weight. She stood with her feet planted wide out, like somebody who tries to keep from a-falling down. Just a trifle back, when I'd talked to her before in this part of the woods, I'd still had my suspicion of her. But now, I began to wonder myself if she wasn't a-saying the truth about how she wanted help.

"I tried to do that thing you told me," she went on, barely to be heard. "I turned aside here where I could hide myself and say a couple prayers. They were hard to say—it's been so long since I prayed to air soul but Satan. I prayed—"

She broke off, her mouth all in a flutter.

"You prayed," I said after her. "All right, what then?"

"I didn't hear me no answer." Again those shaky hands. "John, please take me with you. Hide me."

"You say you're scared to go to your own home."

"Yes. Yes, I am. They'd know I was a-trying to turn myself off from them. They know all sorts of things. John, I can't think where to go, can't think whichaway to turn." Her voice got up shrill and sharp. "What will they do to me?"

"Better not talk so loud," I said, "if you truly don't want them to hear you."

"I'll do aught I can to be right again. I'll go down on my knees, on my face."

"Don't do that here," I said, for she looked ready to fling herself down. I looked her over again, and all of a quick sudden I made up my mind. "Come on along, then," I said.

"Thank you, thank you—"

I headed off again. She started to walk with me, with a kind of stagger to her feet. I heard her breathe, hard and painful.

"I'll let you come with me as far as Mr. Ben's place," I said. "We're a-getting things put in shape for whatever's bound to happen later."

"Thank you, John." Her hand scrabbled at my elbow. "Then you'll let me come in and hide there."

"I nair promised that," I said. "I'll say a word for you. That's all I'll do, all I can do. It's Mr. Ben's home, he's got to suit himself about you."

"Oh." That thought scared her, I could see; or, if she was a-putting on the scare, she was a-doing it as good as an actress on a stage.

We didn't talk after that for a while as we went along and along together. Once or twice we heard little rustly noises back amongst the trees, and Hazel Techeray started at them like a scared rabbit. But naught showed itself in our sight, and I was a right much thankful for that. Finally we came to the place where we could step into the Grays' yard. We stopped under the tall pines at the edge of it.

"Just stand here a second," I bade her, then I raised my voice. "Hello, the house!"

The front door cracked open a bit. "Is that you, John?" said Mr. Ben's voice. "Well, come in out of the heat of this day." Then the door opened itself wider. "Hold on, who's that you got there with you?"

"It's Hazel Techeray," I replied him. "She wants to tell you something."

He stepped into our sight on the porch, his rifle in his hands. "She can go tell it to the jaybirds."

"No, wait just a second," I pleaded for her. "Might could be you'll want to hear this. Might could be it'll pay you to hark to her."

He stood there, strong and still as a rock, for a long, long moment. I heard Hazel Techeray's breath come and go, like somebody near to fall down from a-being tired.

"Hazel Techeray," he gritted at last, "it's a pure waste of both our times, you a-coming here. You're as close to my house as I'll stand for."

"Mr. Ben," I tried one more time, "she's in bad trouble with the Shonokins."

He hawked and spit over the edge of the porch.

"Well, fetch her along in," he said. "But she'd better know, she's a-being watched, air move she makes."

"Come on," I whispered to her, and together we walked to the porch and up the steps and followed Mr. Ben inside.

Callie and Jackson Warren stood back by the sink, a-watching. Neither one of them said a mumbling word. Mr. Ben stood with his rifle tucked under his arm, with his bright eyes narrowed down in his face.

"All right, Hazel Techeray," he said to her, "what's this here thing you got to tell me, and how come you want to tell it?"

"Let me speak a word for her," I offered him, but he shook his gray head no.

"Hold your tater, John. If there's a word to say, she's the one to say it."

With that, Hazel Techeray poured out her whole ugly tale, about how she'd agreed with the Shonokins to give them help; and what the thing was they'd offered in turn. Nor she didn't leave out what she said they wanted of Callie, and how they figured to get their claw-fingered hands on Mr. Ben's alexandrite and rule him by it. We stood and heard her out, Callie in a shiver with big round eyes, Jackson Warren with his mouth drawn as hard and thin as the edge of a knife, Mr. Ben a-holding his rifle and a-scowling and a-swelling.

"I vow and swear," he said when she was done, "if this here's a true fact—and I ain't yet none sure of a word Hazel Techeray says—well, it's just about plenty enough. I ain't a-going to stand for no such things. Ain't no whole peck measure of alexandrites could make me do the like of that."

"You still don't believe me?" Hazel Techeray trembled out at him.

He glowered with both his eyes. "If I was to take what you say without nair proof to it," he said, "hell's gate, it'd be I was as crazy as a pet possum. No, I don't trust you, no way at all. I'd just thank you to get yourself out of this here house of mine."

"Mr. Ben." She looked at him, so pale-faced, so scared. "I only wish you'd point that there gun of yours and shoot me dead."

"I ain't nair yet shot at no woman," he snorted, "and that's a true fact, if air I spoke one on this here earth."

"Then you'll take me and throw me out—"

"No," he said. "I wouldn't lay no hand on you, Hazel Techeray. Ain't a real man's doings to be rough with a woman, and I don't fix to start in with you. But," and he sounded icy-colder with each word of it, "I ain't a-believing in you, neither. I just hark at you and wonder, wonder what you're truly up to with us."

She didn't make him air reply. She sat down in a chair, worn out. She looked over at the stove, where Callie's soup kettle was a-giving off its steam.

"That there smells so good," she kind of sobbed out. "Youins know something, I ain't had me a bite to eat all this day, not even aught for breakfast."

Callie stepped closer to the stove. "Miss Hazel," she said, all of a sudden, "maybe you'd like to have a bowlful of soup."

"Oh, God bless you, Callie Gray!"

Hazel Techeray near about sang those words out into the room. Then she slapped her trembly hand across her mouth.

"Did youins hark at what I said? God bless you, I said. I ain't spoke them words, not in long years."

At last Mr. Ben leaned his gun to the wall beside the closed door. But he still scowled.

Jackson Warren walked over to the shelf where Mr. Ben had his books lined up, and studied them over. Finally he came back to where Hazel Techeray sat. He'd brought along a book with black covers and red edges.

"Miss Techeray," he said to her, as solemn as a judge a-getting ready to pass out a sentence in court, "take this Bible in both your hands and repeat after me what I tell you to say."

She got up out of her chair, a-quivering all over, and took the Bible and held it tight against her crumply blue blouse.

"You want me to take some kind of oath?" she inquired him.

The rest of us stood still and waited, a-wondering ourselves what in the name of gracious he was up to. But he just shook his head, and his tight face loosened itself out into a smile.

"No, ma'am," he said, very quiet. "You don't have to swear anything at all." He smiled wider. "You've proved yourself."

She only gopped at him, as lost as all of us others.

"When you took hold of the Bible," he said, very careful of his words, "when you touched it without any hesitation, you showed you'd given up witchcraft, and that you honestly meant it in your heart. A real witch couldn't have done that. The touch of the Bible would have scorched her fingers."

"I doggies," came out Mr. Ben, deep in his deep chest, "and that there's the God's truth. I done knowed that."

We all of us started a-feeling better, right that moment.

"Then youins believe my word for sure," whimpered Hazel Techeray, and she bent over the old Bible and hugged it to herself like as if it would save her from a-drowning in deep water. "Oh, folks," she said, "this here is a happy moment for me."

"And you said you were hungry," said Callie gently. "Come and sit down at the table."

She ladled out some of the soup into a blue bowl and set it on a corner of the table. She fetched over a spoon and a paper napkin and a square of the cornbread left from what we'd had at lunch. Hazel Techeray sort of whispered out a couple of words, maybe a thank you, and she went to sit herself down and pick up the soup.

"Hold on just a second," said Mr. Ben. "Before you eat, wait."

He tramped to his shelf and got his jug of blockade and poured a good man-sized drink into a glass. He fetched it to Hazel Techeray.

"If you're a-feeling puny, Miss Hazel," he said, "that should ought to help set you right."

That, I told myself, was the first time he hadn't spoken to her, or about her, as Hazel Techeray, her whole name, like the saying of some bad word. He stood beside her and poured himself a good bait, too. The two of them drank together. It was something like what you hear about the old Indians when they smoked a pipe of peace. Hazel Techeray downed her drink like so much water and then she started to go after that soup.

"Why don't I have me some of that, too?" said Mr. Ben. "It does smell right good, daughter. Let's all have us some. It's past five, it's close on to suppertime."

"Let me just keep a watch while the rest of you all eat," I made offer.

The others gathered round to the table. Mr. Ben said him a grace, and they began to eat.

Me, I moved thisaway and that in the room, a-looking out to each side in turn, through the spaces betwixt the logs. The evening sun was bright out yonder, and I saw no movement but the branches of the trees. I went into a back room and had a look out from there, too. No movement behind the house, either. But there was a-going to be something there; there was bound to be. The Shonokins had set things up to come and visit us, and be the worst range of visitors when they did.

The folks talked to one another at the table, just like a bunch of old friends. Didn't say aught about the Shonokins as I recollect, just something about the weather and how crops might come along, the like of that. But I, back in the front room again, had me a look at the guns all leaned against the wall by the door. They were loaded and ready. They said nothing whatever, but they were all set to speak when the speaking time came.

Finally Mr. Ben shoved back his chair and drew in his breath. "I've had me a plenty, John," he said. "Sit down here and have you something, and I'll take on the guard."

"I'll do it with you," said Warren, a-getting up along with Mr. Ben. "Callie, when you're ready to do the dishes, I'll wipe them."

"No, I'll do that," said Hazel Techeray.

By that time, I felt hungry. I was glad to dip me out a

bowl of that soup, red with tomatoes and tangy with onions. It was champion to eat, without salt or either pepper —Callie must have put them in when she mixed it up. As I dipped my spoon in, Callie left the table to look at what was left in the kettle. Hazel Techeray still ate, slowly and carefully, like as if she took note of air spoonful. She looked up at me, some stronger and better-spirited than she'd been up to then.

"How we a-going to face them, John?" she asked me.

"More or less play it by ear, Miss Hazel," I said. "We do know one thing—they can't stand to be killed. Likely they figure to do all the killing that'll be done."

"I'm here to help," she said, quickly, strongly. "I'm one of youins now. When I took that there Bible in my hand, I knew I'd got to be one of you. Mr. Ben can let me have one of them guns."

"I don't reckon to be a-doing that, Miss Hazel," said Mr. Ben, who'd been a-harking at us from over at one side of the room.

She looked at him, a wondering look, a worried look. And he sure enough gave her a smile.

"Not I don't trust you," he said, right gentle in the voice. "I wouldn't have drunk with you nor had soup with you if I didn't trust you. But I'm a-stretching one point to let Callie yonder have a gun with us, and I been a-teaching her how to aim and pull trigger all her life long. These here two men, John and Jackson, they been soldiers in their time and I figure they can be relied on. But you, Miss Hazel, you been a right much excited and stirred up. I don't want to have no gun a-going off at the wrong time and maybe a-hitting the wrong mark."

She gave him a long look, and ducked her head in a nod.

"I see what you mean, Mr. Ben," she said. "Likely there's a lot in what you say."

"I hope and trust I'm right," he said. "If I know the first thing about what we're up against, I figure it for the biggest danger I ever seen; and I seen enough danger in my time to last a healthy man a hundred long years."

"Yes, sir," she said. "What must I do?"

"You ask John that; he's the captain."

"Help us," I told her. "Take a turn at the watch. Maybe you can figure on some of the Shonokin doings. That'll be good on our side."

Hazel Techeray and I finished eating. We carried our dishes to the sink. Callie and Warren had started in to wash up there, a-talking while they did that, but Hazel Techeray took the towel from Warren and said she'd help Callie. Warren didn't look whole-souled about quitting, but he went to watch at the back. Mr. Ben beckoned me over by the door.

"Here's the situation as I see it," he said. "They'll be a-coming here. Likely they're on their way now. If they wait for night, at least we'll have some part of a moon up there to help us. Now, we've all said you're in command. How do we handle it?"

"Keep quiet and keep the lights down," I said. "One lamp at the dimmest it can be burned. There are five of us now—that should give two of us lying-down time now and then to rest while the other three use round the house and spy out for Shonokins. Make as little noise as possible. And not a shot fired without a-being sure it'll smack home."

"Smack home," he said the words after me, and he truly seemed to love to say them. "Maybe wait till they're almost up against the house, and then let them have it where they're biggest."

"One thing Hazel Techeray said," I reminded him. "About your alexandrite. They want to get hold of it. They reckon it'll give them command over you."

"All right, it stays right here in my pocket," he said, and slapped the place.

"No, hold on," I said, and made up my mind as I spoke. "Likely they'll do what they can to lay hold on you and get it away from you. That thing should be put somewhere else, where they wouldn't count on it being."

"Where?"

"Let me take it." I held out my hand, and he passed it over. A beam of sunlight came through a space in the logs and made it glitter green. I tore off a scrap of a paper napkin and rolled the thing up in that, and stowed it deep in the pocket of my own old pants.

"They purely want that alexandrite, and they figure on a-getting it from you," I said. "But now, if they lay hold on you, you won't have it. And let them try to get it from me, even if they find out I've got it."

"That's a good notion, John," he said. "All right, let them try their tricks on me. They can kill me, but they can't scare me."

And dogged if he didn't say it the way you'd figure he purely meant it.

Callie and Hazel Techeray were a-finishing up the dishes. Warren looked from a rear door and looked at Callie, and she knew he was a-looking. She sang a few words of a song, "Little Margaret" as I recollect, and he tried to sing it with her, not as tuneful as she was.

"Callie," he said, "when this business is over, you and I ought to sit down together and make a book of the songs you know. I know some publishers."

"I'd love to, Jackson," she said back to him.

And no doubt in her voice but that this would be all over and the two of them could do that thing. When they talked thataway, it made me feel better about the trouble we were in, betwixt the rock and the hard place, you might call it; and about how we could figure to win out some way.

Hazel Techeray came to where I was. That good soup and that sup of blockade had done wonders for her. She stepped stronger and her face wasn't so peaked up.

"Those young folks are in love," she whispered me.

"I do truly think they are," I said.

"It's right good to see them. Good to think what's ahead for them—" She broke off. "Whatever can be ahead for them, if the Shonokins come?"

"The Shonokins will come all right, Miss Hazel," I said, "but maybe we can show them a quick way back from here."

"How?"

"We'll do it," I said, a-wondering how.

Mr. Ben had sat himself down by the fireplace. He had the Bible that Warren had used to show us how Hazel Techeray had stopped from her witchcraft ways. "Me," he said, "I'll just cast the signs to see what to do."

I'd seen that trick of old folks, how you open the Bible three times just by chance and put your finger each time on a text. Mr. Ben flopped the Bible open on his knee and stabbed down with his finger.

"Here we are," he allowed. "Hark at this: 'Whoever perished, being innocent? Or where were the righteous cut off?' "

"That's out of the Book of Job," I said, "and I sure enough hope it's true, and I hope we've got the innocence and righteousness to qualify."

"Amen," said Hazel Techeray.

Mr. Ben opened the Bible again. "What youins reckon this here might could mean? 'The horseleech hath two daughters, crying Give, give.' " He gave us all a look. "That there's one of the Proverbs, but how you a-going to get action on it?"

"Horseleech," Hazel Techeray said after him. "Once I heard tell, that means a vampire."

"I've heard the same," said Jackson Warren.

"One more time now." Mr. Ben had the Bible open farther along. He read out loud: " 'When it is evening, ye say, It will be fair weather; for the sky is red.' "

He got up and put the Bible back in its place on the shelf. We watched while he walked to the western wall and peeked out through a crack betwixt the logs.

"The sun's a-fixing to go down red," he said. "A-fixing to be fair weather, all right."

Then he shoved closer to the wall. "Ladies and men," he said, "ain't only sunset out there, but I think I see something on the move, behind them trees at the edge of the yard."

I jumped to a place beside him and looked out, too.

I made out the trees, the ground, the bright red of the sun a-going down. Then something else.

A streak of flame shot up from a dark place in the pines, sailed at the house and up above it.

"What was that?" I said.

"By God, a fire arrow," yelled Mr. Ben. "They done set them an arrow on fire and shot it up on the roof."

XII

Then we all of us stood still and quiet, the whole bunch of us, for seconds. All of a sudden I heard, or reckoned I heard, a sound of crackling. The sound of wood caught afire.

"They're a-going to burn us out!" moaned Hazel Techeray, and she hung with both her hands to the back of a chair. "They'll drive us out of here into the open, get us where they'll do us however they want to do!"

"I'll be go to hell if they do," said Mr. Ben. "Me, I'm a-going to get up yonder on the roof, and I'll—"

"You hold on there, Mr. Ben!" I yelled at him, so loud he stopped right in his tracks. "I'll tend to this matter. A plate, where's a plate, somebody?"

"A plate, John?" said Callie, like as if she wondered herself what I meant, but she ran and fetched me one and put it on the table, a plate of blue plastic.

I grabbed me hold of a pencil and I wrote on it. The pencil made faint letters, but plain enough to read, the old magic square I knew by heart:

$$\begin{matrix} S & A & T & O & R \\ A & R & E & P & O \\ T & E & N & E & T \\ O & P & E & R & A \\ R & O & T & A & S \end{matrix}$$

Those strange words, that read the same backward or forward, or up and down. . . . Then I whipped the plate over quick and set the same letters on the bottom of it. I grabbed it and ran for the back room where the ladder was.

"It's almighty dark up in that there loft," said Mr. Ben, right behind me.

"I told you, let me tend to this," I said to him, and I purely sailed up that ladder. In the blackness of the loft, I had to grope up over my head for the rafters, but I found the roof trapdoor and flung it up. Loud sounded that crackly fire, like corn a-popping. The red light of it showed me the place to shove my head and shoulders up into the open.

It was bright fire, sure enough, all against the darkening night sky, a big blaze of it on the broad old home-split shakes of the roof. I held the plate with its letters in both my hands, and I shouted out something else I recollected from *The Long Lost Friend:*

"Our dear Sarah journeyed through the land, having a fiery hot brand in her hand," I repeated over, loud as I could. "The fiery brand heats, the fiery brand sweats. Fiery brand, stop your heat; fiery brand, stop your sweat."

And with that, I flung the plate right where the fire was the hottest-looking.

Right off that quick while I watched, the flames drew all down and disappeared away. I wondered myself, as at times before, if the Sarah in the charm meant Sarah, the wife of Abraham and the mother of Isaac. Or was it like I'd heard somewhere from somebody, it might could mean Seraph, a holy angel. I looked out. Not air spark showed itself now. The fire had gone plumb out. I looked one more time, to make sure, and got back down.

"What was that there thing you said?" Mr. Ben inquired me in the dark of the loft.

I dragged the trapdoor back into its place. "Just a thing to douse out the fire and keep it doused," was all I could reply to him. "Let's go back down there again, and see what they'll try to do to us next."

He climbed down the ladder and I followed after him. All the others sort of goggled us in the front room. "What happened?" asked Jackson Warren.

"John here just done put that fire arrow of theirs clean out of business," said Mr. Ben, and smacked his hand down hard on my shoulder.

"And it'll stay out," I added to that, sure of what I said. "The same way that witchcraft stuff was taken off this place. Whatever the Shonokins want to do to us, they've got to do it some natural way of doing."

"Oh," breathed Callie, "how can we thank you, John?"

"Don't thank me," I said. "Thank the man that wrote that old book of mine, *The Long Lost Friend*."

I went and poured me a cup of strong black coffee from the pot on the stove. It was right scaldy all the way down, but it made me feel better. It took out the shake from me that that business on the roof had given me.

"All right, now," I said. "What are they up to out in the yard?"

Jackson Warren had gone to a place where he could see out betwixt logs. He held his rifle ready. "Nothing that I can see," he reported me, "and there's moon enough by now that I think I could see them if they came into the open."

"They ain't about to come into the open," sniffed out Mr. Ben. "If they done that, I'd give them another dead Shonokin to scare the hell out of them."

"Callie, will you go watch at the back of the house?" I said. "You two men, keep guard at the two side walls in here. I'm a-going to holler out yonder and talk to them."

"You be almighty careful, John," Mr. Ben warned at me.

"The thought of a-being careless hasn't nair entered my head," I told him.

I went to the front door and dragged it open a few inches. I could feel Hazel Techeray a-looking at my back. I stood close to the open space.

"Hello, out there yonder!" I yelled. "Speak up and tell us what you think you want."

"We don't want you, John," came back the voice I well knew belonged to Brook Altic. "We want Ben Gray to do whatever talking is to be done."

"I'm a-doing the talking for in here," I called into the early dark. "Do you have a word to say? Say it, and I'll hark at it."

"Then come out on the porch with your hands up," he said. I had him figured to be some good way into the front yard, likely behind a big tree or some other thing to hide him from air shot.

"I said I'd hark at you," I called again. "I nair said I'd do what you ordered me. I'm nair such a gone gump as to come out yonder."

"You can never get away, John. None of you can get away. We've got you penned up in that little cabin."

I let myself laugh at that. "Now, whoever said we wanted to come out? It's nice in here, Brooke Altic. We've got meal in the barrel, meat on the hook, water in the bucket, and fire in the stove. We can do all right inside here. We've likewise got guns, in case you don't know that, and if you crowd us just one little bitty bit we may show you the color of Shonokin blood."

"That's a-telling them good, John," muttered Mr. Ben at my side.

Mr. Brooke Altic didn't say a word for a few moments

then. Likely he busied himself to chew on what I'd said. Then:

"John, you're in a trap. You and everybody with you. You're most tightly shut up in your little shed. It's dark now, it's our time. We have various ways of getting at you that you don't dream of. So come out with your hands up. All of you."

"What if we don't?" I asked into the falling darkness.

"Then you'll earnestly wish you had. I promise you that you'll wish you had."

"If you come a-fooling with us," I said back, "you'll do some wishing yourself, will wish you hadn't. You've already tried fire and it didn't work. Right this minute," I said, "none of your crowd has the guts to step out where a fair shot can be had at him."

"You seem to be talking as though for everybody there inside," said Brooke Altic, "but you and I aren't talking at all profitably. Let me say a word to Ben Gray."

Ben Gray was right there beside me. "Here I am, Brooke Altic," he hollered past me. "Here I am, a-hungering for a sight of you out in the open, and what you got to answer me back?"

"I think you have a reasonable mind, Mr. Gray," said Brooke Altic's voice from wherever he was hid, in his way that made him sound so reasonable himself. "I despair of John, for whom I had hoped to do so much. You're more apt to listen to the voice of sense, even though you killed one of us."

"He asked for it," said Mr. Ben. "He was a-trying to kill me."

"He only wanted your jewel, your alexandrite."

"And he nair got none of it, did he?"

"Mr. Gray," said Brooke Altic, "you and I can come to a sensible agreement here. Take that jewel and wrap it up in a handkerchief, something white. Throw it out here into the yard where we can get it. And in exchange for that, I'll engage to do you favors in a hundred different ways—"

"That there's enough of that," busted in Mr. Ben. "I don't want no more of such fine talk from you. If you hanker for my alexandrite, or aught else I've got, come try to take it and see what you wind up a-getting instead."

Another of Altic's waits before he made an answer. Then: "Mr. Gray, you make yourself sound as intransigent as John himself. Suppose we wait a short while here and give you time to come to your senses."

"Hell's brass gates, you can wait till you're splayfooted and jimberjawed," Mr. Ben yelled right back to him. "I've spoken my piece and I'll stick to it."

He pulled back away from the door and walked to where his jug stood. "I need a grain of blockade to take the taste of that no-good Shonokin out of my mouth," he allowed, and poured him a thimbleful. He took it down in one quick catch, and I saw his eye to glitter in the soft light in there.

"Lord have mercy," he said, "maybe I talked to him all wrong."

"You talked to him all right, Mr. Ben," said Hazel Techeray. "I done already told you how come him to want that alexandrite thing, use it to order you round. It wouldn't nair do to give it to him."

"What I mean is, I could have made off to give it to him," he said. "I should ought to have talked like as if I agreed him, and then flung out a white cloth without the alexandrite, and stood by to plug whichever of them tried to pick it up. Maybe it ain't too late yet, maybe if I said I'd change my mind, didn't mean them things I said, then—"

"I fear that won't work, Mr. Ben," I had to say. "The

way you got him told, he'd know you meant that thing. He'd figure a trick and be a-looking out for it."

"Well then, all right," he agreed me. "I'll let him have the thing how I laid it out to him. Let him come and try something on here. It'll be like to crawl down a black bear's mouth to take his food away from him."

I let things stand at that. I told Mr. Ben to sit down and rest, maybe have another taste of that good soup, while Jackson Warren and I watched the different sides of the cabin. I picked up the rifle that had been laid out for me, though I didn't purely want to. And I made Callie to come into the front room, too. She and Hazel Techeray got a-talking things, the sort of things women talk, like as if they were on a visit together. Outside was the deadest quiet. I wondered if sure enough Brooke Altic was a-waiting for his words to sink into us.

I think it was some spell of time before one of us spoke on the fix we were in. It was Hazel Techeray.

"Mr. Ben," she said, "I've come to the same thought as you and John. It wouldn't be no point in a-throwing out a white cloth to them. They'd know right well you'd not put your jewel into it."

"I been a-thinking that same thing," Mr. Ben agreed her.

From outside came Brooke Altic's voice from somewhere near:

"Hazel Techeray? Hazel Techeray?"

"Don't you reply him," I whispered her, and went to where I could spy out betwixt two logs. I saw trees and some of the open ground, sort of washed pale by the light of the moon, but no movement in it. If I'd seen that, I'd have fired at it with my gun.

"Hazel Techeray," said Brooke Altic, "come out to us.

We know you're in there. Out here, we know everything you say or do, as soon as you speak or move."

I glanced round at her. She was pushed so low down in her chair, she near about fell out of it. She was close to a faint.

"You've been a sad fool, Hazel," Brooke Altic said to her, his voice all drawn out to carry inside to us. "I hadn't truly thought that of you. But come out of there. We're still quite willing to do all we promised for you, give you the honor and preferment we offered you. Come out, I say."

"No!" she screeched out, high and shrill as a note on a bugle.

She had jumped up on her feet. She rocked back and forth, and put her hand on the chair back to hold herself steady.

"I ain't a-going to do it, I won't do what you tell me to!" she hollered, loud enough to be heard all the way to the county seat. "You can't make me!"

Silence again, while you might could have counted a slow six. I could hear myself breathe where I watched.

"Then I'll stop trying to talk sense to you, Hazel," came Brooke Altic's voice at last. "But I still offer reasonable terms to everyone else there in that cabin. As for you, I wash my hands of you. We all wash our hands of you. Ben Gray and John had better wash their hands of you."

Hazel Techeray let go the grab she had on the chair. She started to walk toward the door, slow as somebody in a dream. Mr. Ben jumped to her side and took hold of her arm.

"Don't you nair think of a-going out to them," he said in her ear.

"If I did, maybe youins would be better off," she mumbled back to him.

"Don't you nair believe for a second we'll be better off,"

he said back. "But if you was to go out yonder to them, you'd be another sight worse off. You done heard what Brooke Altic said about that."

"Well, if I can sure enough stay in here—"

"I done already said you could," he broke in, "and what I say is what I mean."

I harked at all their talk while I watched out toward the side and front of the house. Jackson Warren sort of kept up a tour here and yonder, and he came to my side and peeked through the space.

"I think I make out one of them in that little string of bushes," he said under his breath, and fetched up his rifle to aim. But I grabbed it and pushed it back down.

"No, hold your fire," I told him. "Let's not send them a shot till we can be certain sure it's smack in the bull's-eye."

"I could hit one of them from here by this light," he argued.

"You've got to kill with a shot," I said. "A-killing one is what we've got to study to do."

Kill. We were down to that. Kill something, that was the way of mankind.

Again I had that thought about the cruelty and selfishness in the whole history of this world. Man had got rule of the world, or anyway he reckoned he had, not a-being aware of how the Shonokins felt about it. And man had killed and killed. Not only other men. There wasn't one kind of animal he'd spared without a selfish thought about it. Folks talk and talk about kindness to animals, sure enough. But we're kind to horses because they work for us, cattle because they give us meat and milk, sheep because they have wool, dogs because they'll hunt for us and bark strangers off from the door. Even cats, because they look pretty a-sitting by the fire. Other than that—man has killed off things like buffalo and passenger pigeons; he catches fish by the twenties and flings them on the bank. He burns down forests, dirties the rivers and the lakes. Man doesn't have half sense. And to settle things with other men—well, that comes out to more killing.

"Hold it till you have a center shot," I warned Jackson Warren again.

And there I was, a-doing the same thing, a-fixing to kill Shonokins. And how about the Shonokins, who wanted to rule instead of man? Did they have enough of man nature in them to settle it all by kill, kill, kill?

The night outside seemed to get just a tad darker as I kept my watch, my own gun in my hand.

It was some time along later, maybe past nine o'clock as Jackson Warren said by his watch. We'd taken our turns on guard a couple of times. Now it was Hazel Techeray in one of the back rooms, and Ben Gray a-squinting out at the front. Callie and Warren and I sat at the table, a-having the first cups from a fresh pot of coffee. I'd dipped out a little more soup, and I relished that.

Then, thunk! Something hit hard on the front wall. Thunk! Something else hit close to the first. I jumped up quick to find out what.

Ben Gray was at a space in the logs.

"They're a-trying those devilish fire arrows again," he said.

I opened the door a couple of inches and looked to see.

Both their arrows had driven into the logs under the porch roof, and they burned bright all along the lengths of their shafts. But they didn't set air blaze to the logs. I watched, and they died down. *The Long Lost Friend* still shielded us.

"I'm afraid we must burn you out of there," called the voice of Brooke Altic from a dark place.

"Don't hold your breath till it happens," I called back. "We've got your fire stopped."

"Might I be allowed to come and talk to you?" he asked.

"If you come into sight with your hands up, all right," I said. "Just you by yourself, none of that trouble gang you've got with you. But I'll guarantee your talking won't get you much."

"On second thought," he said, "I don't think I'll come in sight of you, John. Somehow I don't feel as if you're to be trusted."

"That makes it unanimous," I replied him. "I wouldn't trust you air farther than a toad can spit."

By then, I reckoned, I was a-talking as mean to him as Ben Gray his own self. I waited for him to reply me. Again he took him several seconds before he did.

"John," he said my name, "I do hope you enjoyed the beautiful sunrise this morning. Because it's the last one you'll ever see."

"I'll be a-seeing tomorrow's sunrise," I made the promise. "And day after tomorrow's sunrise, and more to come, if the good Lord spares me."

"Don't call on the Lord to spare you, John," said Brooke Altic, hard as a frozen rock. "Don't call on me to spare you, either. We bide our time here, but we'll husk you and your friends out of that cabin like nuts out of their shells."

"And here we sit and wait for you to try it on," I said. "We banter you to try it on. We're ready for you to try it on."

"Wait and find out."

As his voice trailed off on that, it sounded sort of tired.

I shoved the door all the way back shut. The others looked at me, looked at one another. They'd been a-harking, and all but Hazel Techeray had harked with a gun at the ready.

"Again you spoke him your piece right," said Mr. Ben to me.

"By now," I hoped, "we may have spoken all the pieces we've got to speak. I'm tired of a-talking. It'll maybe be some kind of action from this on out."

"What will they do?" asked Callie from one of the rear doors.

"Whatever they do, we'll contrive to counterpunch them," Warren said, like as if he'd figured out how.

"I tell you again, if they come into the open, hold your fire till they get in close enough to stop a plumb-center shot," I warned them. "It won't help us to just wound one. They've got to have a corpse on their hands to be sure enough scared out."

Outside somewhere at the front, rose the note of a whippoorwill. *Whi-ah-whoo*, it said, *whi-ah-whoo*.

"Sounds to me like some devilish old Shonokin a-signaling," whispered Mr. Ben.

"Sounds to me like just only a whippoorwill," I said.

Whi-ah-whoo, whi-ah-whoo, came from out yonder in front. I went to look through a space thataway.

Something little and dark seemed like as if it crept along in the road, where the moonlight filtered down.

"I see it," said Warren's voice beside me.

Next second, before I could raise a hand to stop him, he shoved his rifle through the space in the logs and fired.

"I done told you not to do that," I scolded at him.

That little dark thing had spun over and over and lay still as a stone. He'd hit it where it lived. Then we heard a laugh.

"Really and truly," came a-mocking the voice of Brooke Altic, "that was cruel of you, John, or whoever fired. Snuffing out the life of a poor, pitiful little whippoorwill, when it was only trying to find a bug for its poor, pitiful little supper. The humane society would have something un-pleasant to say to you."

"At least you know that we're ready to shoot," barked out Jackson Warren.

Brooke Altic laughed again. "Ah, a new voice heard from."

"My name's Jackson Warren," said Warren. "Why don't you show yourself? You'd be considerably easier to hit than a bird."

"Jackson Warren," Brooke Altic repeated him. "I've heard that name, I believe."

"I've helped a man named Thunstone against you."

"Yes, of course. Hello, Mr. Warren. Good-bye, Mr. Warren."

Warren slewed round to point his rifle to where the voice came, but I grabbed his shoulder and yanked him away from the wall.

"You hold your fire till I give you an order," I said, "or you and I are a-going to have trouble."

He scowled in the soft light, but he moved back. Silence again, except only for Hazel Techeray. She mumbled and mumbled where she sat in her chair. All of a sudden she got up.

We others stood and gopped at her while she stood there; for she stood proud again, strong again, the way I'd seen her stand when first I came up on her in that clearing in the woods behind Mr. Ben's place. She flung her arms out sideways, like the arms of a cross.

"I made my wish before this," she rattled out the same words I'd heard her say that morning. "I make it now. There was no day I didn't see my wish fulfilled—"

Then she went silent as a graveyard on a dark night. Her arms dropped to her sides. She slumped herself down, like a flag when the wind dies out of it. Her head bowed. Her hair looked tired on her head.

"I can't make it work," she whimpered.

"Sure you can't," I said. "You quit a-being a witch. Nair spell will work for you now. You shouldn't ought to try."

"But I was a-trying to do good for us with it," she halfway shed tears to say. "While Brooke Altic was a-talking to Mr. Warren, I said me a spell on him."

"Ain't we had us a good old horse doctor's dose of spells?" wondered Mr. Ben from where he stood on watch next the door. "Ain't we near about ready to trust in powder and lead and maybe God up in heaven?"

Hazel Techeray stumbled back again to her chair and sat down. She near about fell out of it as she fell into it.

"I said a spell that should have killed Brooke Altic dead in his tracks," she blubbered. "And it didn't." Her face twitched. "It didn't do no such thing."

"Miss Hazel, you're through with spells," I said to her. "Anyhow, it wouldn't work, with what I did here to put off witch spells."

"You're right, John, and I reckon I did wrong to try it," she moaned. "I was just only a-trying to help out the only way I knew."

All this went on in the dimmest softest of light in that room, from the turned-down lamp in the corner. Likely we were darker inside there than the Shonokins outside. And better off, too. The death of one of us wouldn't whip us, the way the death of one of them would whip them.

A sort of wind came a-rising up. We could hear it out yonder amongst the trees. It pushed against the front of the house, pushed harder. Callie came into the front room, and her eyes were big, the way they could get big.

"We're about to have a storm," she said.

"A storm made by Shonokins," I guessed.

"This might could be called a natural wind," I said, a-harking to it. "Made by some natural power. Just now, the Shonokins are at the edge of this property. Likely they're a-running their power line right across some of Mr. Ben's land, legal or not."

The wind started in to shriek outside. It rattled those planks we'd nailed at the window. It sniffed and shoved at the door, like some big old thing that wanted to come in.

Outside there, above all the noise of the blowing, rose up another noise, loud and wailing.

It was the Shonokins, a-laughing about it.

XIII

Gentlemen, that was a storm for whosoever might could call for one. The wind came a-howling through those spaces betwixt the logs in the walls, would have blown out our lamp if it hadn't been set in a corner, with a chimney and shade to it. That wind grabbed on to the house and pulled it back and forth and near to round about, like as if it wanted to drag us up by the roots. Then came rain, a flood of it like from a bunch of fire hoses. Rain came in through the log spaces along with the wind. And in a minute, hail, a rattling, pounding bait of hail, a-popping on the logs and roof-shakes like the Devil's own personal buckshot, like dice a-tumbling in the Devil's favorite cup.

I saw the dim lamplight flicker on Mr. Ben's strong-lined face. He downright grinned across the room at us.

"This here cabin has stood up under worse storms," he said, loud enough to be heard over all the racket. "My old folks built it on a rock, same as that house they tell in the Bible. Hell, I even been out in worse than this in my time."

As I harked to him, I wondered if I'd been out in worse. Maybe I had been, once off at the war. I recollected the rain that long-ago night, a-soaking me down to my underwear, a-running into my combat boots, the rain and the wind that awful night. And the mortar shells a-busting here and there, near and far round me, and the mean, streaking cuts of tracers all over like fireflies. It had been like a dress rehearsal for the day of judgment. I wondered myself if that storm had been as bad as this loud one on us now.

"We're in the hands of God," said Callie to Warren, loud enough for us all to hear her.

"Oh yes," Hazel Techeray wept, off by herself.

"And I sure enough hope you're right on that, daughter," spoke up Mr. Ben. "I hope God ain't took off the night and left things to the cheap help."

Just right then, quick as it had come on us, that quick the storm was gone. The wind dropped dead, the rain and the slam-down beat of the hail stopped themselves. Silence fell on us, so purely complete you could hear it a-being silent. You asked yourself what had happened to the noise. You could have heard a pin drop, if somebody had dropped a pin.

Warren went to a chink in the logs and put his eye to it.

"A spell brought that on," he said.

"Spell?" Hazel Techeray echoed him. "But—but—"

"The protective spell John said may not work against everything," he said. "Storms can be raised. Guazzo tells us about them in his *Demonalotry* book."

"Shoo," I said. "One time way out west, I saw me some Indians dance and sing and pray to bring rain down when they were a-hurting for it. And it looked to be a natural thing to me."

Outside, a drawling, teasing voice: "Hello, the house again!"

It made me mad. I drifted to a log space. "Hello yourself, Brooke Altic," I called into the night.

"Is that you, John? How did you like our little operatic performance?"

"For the beginning of the overture, it was right amusing," I said. "You know, Mr. Altic, you just fixed yourselves so there's no point in using fire arrows anymore. The logs and the roof must be soaked as wet as sop."

"By the ones I worship, you may be right," came his drawl. "We live and learn, don't we, John? But I don't want to talk to you. Let me address myself to lovely little Callie Gray."

"I won't say one word to him," she whispered.

"Don't," said Warren, from where he kept his lookout, gun in hand.

We waited and said naught.

"Miss Callie Gray," said Altic's slow voice, "I'm driven to wonder if you may not be the only rational person in that beleaguered house. I'd like to say to you, this whole little incident might turn out to your advantage."

She didn't speak. Not one of us spoke.

"Callie Gray, you could make yourself happy among us," said Altic's voice. "You could be prosperous among us, you could be fruitful among us—"

"That will do out there," yelled Warren at him, mad enough to sting like a hornet.

"Do I hear the voice of Jackson Warren?"

"You don't hear the voice of Callie Gray," came back Warren. "She knows all about those plans you want to make for her."

"All about them?" Altic mocked him.

"Yes, she does, and she's not having any."

A laugh out there. "I suppose you have the right to speak for her."

"I'm doing it."

Callie had moved up behind Warren, and she put her hand on his arm. It was pretty to see her do that thing, in the dim light.

"Now, then," came Altic's mockery-sounding voice,

"you think you've said enough, do you? You think we'll just quit and go away? Leave you alone?"

"We don't think nair such thing," Mr. Ben told him from where he stood to look out another place. "We think you'll use round out there till one of you gets out in the open and we can take a fair shot at him."

Brooke Altic laughed his laugh. "You ask too much from us, Mr. Gray, a whole lot too much. Various things will happen without that happening. We've just begun to open our bag of tricks." He paused. "Of course, you can get rid of us by throwing that alexandrite out to us."

"Don't hold your breath a-waiting that long," Mr. Ben spit out.

Thunder rolled fit to bust your ears just then, and a bright flash of lightning flung a moment of white fire in at all the log spaces.

"That near about hit the place," gulped Hazel Techeray, scared.

Another thunder roll, another white fiery flash that came in and lighted up the whole room for a second.

"They'll blast this house down." Hazel Techeray was near about a-sobbing.

"Not them," I said to calm her down. "They want us alive or, at least, some of us."

No more thunder after that. The silence came a-creeping back in round us. Finally Altic's voice from outside broke that silence.

"You people simply won't listen to reason," he said, like as if he mourned at it, from somewhere close to the side of the cabin.

I pushed over close to the wall at that point and looked out. The moon showed itself again, and maybe two-three stars, and I saw just a big pine tree. Likely he was behind that, within feet of where I stood. I poked my rifle through the logs.

"We'll always listen to reason," I said. "That's how come there's no point to listen to you."

"John," he mocked. "Oh, John, John. You're a thorn in the flesh of progress, John. The United States Government would never like what I could say about you."

"Get the government in here to hark at both sides of the story," I said.

"John," he said my name again, "you have a lost cause. As lost as the cause of the old Confederacy. By now, we've brought our line of power to this point. We can do whatever we want to with you."

I decided not to swap words with him on that. He sounded another sight readier of tongue than what I was. I looked out there at his tree. The rifle Mr. Ben had given me would have slapped a bullet all the way through it, but just to wound Altic wouldn't finish him. We had to have a Shonokin dead.

I heard a creaky, grinding sound, and the house shifted on its foundation rocks. It was like something with water a-pushing it in a flood. Hazel Techeray made one of her whimpers again. Callie said, "What in the name of gracious?" And Mr. Ben said something I'd bet he wouldn't want written down as his last words in this life.

I peeked out again. The trees in the yard waved their branches like arms and I heard the whipping rustle of their leaves. The house creaked. Gentlemen, it was a mean night on us there.

For, as I reckoned, the Shonokins had somehow or other put their line of power along the ground to us like a gun aimed to a target. They wanted to scare us right out into the open. If that happened, what would come next?

I couldn't reply myself on that, so I didn't try.

Yet again I took a squint. Out yonder, something sort of scuttered amongst some bushes. I aimed the best I could and touched my trigger. The rifle banged.

"Yow!" came a howl to answer it. Mr. Ben edged along toward me.

"I got him, I think," I whispered. "I hope."

There was a low muttering sound here and there, like voices. I heard a rattle of leaves, where maybe something was a-being dragged. I had a hope for what it was.

But then, Altic's voice came again, his drawly, mocking voice again.

"That was only a slight flesh wound on a friend of mine. Let me make a last offer before we throw that place down on top of you fools. All of you can come out and be safe, except John."

"They want to kill you, John," Hazel Techeray whispered me.

"All except John," said Altic again. "Come out without weapons, and you can leave along the road. Leave safely, leave alive. Just give us that alexandrite. That's a promise on the spirit we Shonokins worship. When I say that, you know I mean what I say."

"Miss Hazel's right," said Mr. Ben. "They're a-fixing to kill you, John."

"Kill John, and nobody else," Warren added on. "They want to save the rest of us for purposes of their own. If we stay in here, they won't try to smash us with the house."

"Well, don't say aught back to them," said Mr. Ben.

The house gave itself a grind again. We felt a shove all round us, like as if the air had gone as heavy as water. The stout old rafters above our heads creaked in their fastenings.

"Do you understand that we mean exactly what we say?" called Brooke Altic to us.

I held up my hands for all to be quiet, say naught. Well I knew that if we didn't reply him, Brooke Altic would have something else to say. That would slow up what he was a-trying to trick on us. It might even tip his hand. We waited and, sure enough, there came his voice again.

"I've asked several times for that jewel, that alexandrite. Let me say, I'll make a fair exchange for it—more than a fair exchange, a liberal one. I have here a ring set with a ten-carat diamond, and all around the diamond are arranged ten fine rubies. It's worth a fortune." His voice rose up. "What do you say to that offer, Mr. Ben Gray?"

"Don't talk no offer to me," said Mr. Ben, before I could hush him. "I ain't got it no more, nohow."

"Who does have it, then?" Altic inquired him from the dark yard.

"That there comes under the head of it's you to find out."

"Very well. My offer stands, though; this valuable ring for that semiprecious stone. Do I hear a reply?"

Again I had my hand up to keep them all quiet.

"I see. I suppose that silence means bleak refusal. Then you have only yourselves to thank for what will happen now. My profound regrets."

He went quiet, and we felt what we'd felt before, that grinding press of power all over the house. Our lamp tottered where we'd set it, might could have tipped over if Hazel Techeray hadn't caught it up with both hands. The rafters creaked and popped so loud, I wondered if they weren't just before a-coming down. And I felt a feeling I'd known before: a hum in my blood with a sing in my ears, the same way as I'd felt them out on that straight-drawn trail to the Shonokin settlement.

There was a burny feeling on my right leg, on the outside of it just below the hip. I thought a spark must have come there to me from somewhere, and I slapped at it.

"What is it, John?" said Callie to me. "Did something hit you?"

"I don't rightly know," I said with my hand to the place. It felt warm there, but no sure-enough fire to it. "I can't say for certain what it is."

The cabin settled out of its wigglings. The tingle left out of me. I dived my hand into my pants pocket and fetched out the alexandrite in its little twist of paper and unwrapped it a trifle bit. It showed pale in our dim light. And it felt warm.

I walked over close to where Hazel Techeray still held our lamp. Jackson Warren came across to my side. He poked at the wadded paper.

"It feels almost hot enough to catch fire," he said. "That's the alexandrite, isn't it, John?"

"Right, and they're getting their power line to it somehow."

"I can see one of them a-scrambling round out yonder," said Mr. Ben from where he was on watch.

I set the thing down on the edge of the table and near about ran to the place. I looked out betwixt the logs.

And sure enough, there was movement in a shadowy place in the yard near the path, where some bushes grew. A dark patch the size of a man, or maybe a little bear. It hung low. It twitched itself thisaway and that.

"Just let me, by God, get him in my sights," rumbled Mr. Ben, and he ran his gun barrel through the space to take aim.

"Hold your fire, Ben Gray!" sort of wailed somebody out in the dark yard.

"Sim Drogus, as I live and draw breath," said Mr. Ben.

I saw the dark shape rise up and stretch its hands above its head.

"Hold your fire," said Sim Drogus again. "I've come here to do you some good, Mr. Ben."

"If you come here to do me good, it's the first damn time," Mr. Ben gritted back at him. "What you got to say to me? Speak it out, and make it short."

"Come out at the door," Sim Drogus asked him.

"Come out and be a target for your Shonokin friends? My mother nair raised me to be air such a fool. I'll come to the door and talk to you through it, and you come along to where I can see you plain."

All us others in the house started to crowd round. I waved for them to get back and stay on watch. Mr. Ben stamped hard to the door and pulled it a couple inches open with the muzzle of his rifle. I was close enough to see out at a chink to the front.

It was sure enough Sim Drogus who came along the path toward the steps. I knew him by his slumpy shoulders, his long skinny neck. He stood almost at the foot of the steps.

"Mr. Ben," he said, "I done come here with a friendly message for you, from Mr. Brooke Altic."

"Hagh!" snorted Mr. Ben, like a mean horse. "Me and him is through with aught you could call friendly. And you, how come you not to be a-running to the law with word of shooting here? You're right good at that."

I saw Sim Drogus sort of twitch and sway himself, like as if he felt embarrassed.

"Mr. Ben," he tried again, "you well know I nair carried no tale on you to them deputies. It was Hazel Techeray. You got her in there right this minute, and if she's honest she'll tell you the same. Anyhow, ain't no other neighbor round these parts is close enough to hark at this fuss you're a-raising up."

"Hagh!" Mr. Ben snorted at him again. "Them toredown Shonokins you got is a-raising the fuss, and none of them dare step forward to me, so they send you. You're their little fetch-and-carry dog, ain't you, now?"

"Go on, cuss me out if that pleasures you," said Sim Drogus. He had his hands up. "I won't hold that hard against you, if you cuss me out. But I'm come to be a peacemaker betwixt you and Mr. Altic. My message is, he only wants to make you rich, make you happy. He wants just one little teeny thing from you."

"You come on up here and step inside my door, Sim Drogus," invited Mr. Ben, with meanness in air word, "and I'll write out an answer to that there message. Right on your weasel face, one that Brooke Altic could read by the moonlight. If your Shonokin friends wasn't there to help you, I'd come outside and run you right up the tallest tree there is in miles."

"You won't listen to reason?" asked Sim Drogus, the same way Brooke Altic had asked.

"I won't listen to you and that's the naked truth. Now then, I'm a-going to count three for you to get out of my sight."

"I'm sorry for you, Ben Gray," squeaked Sim Drogus, and he turned round and made off quick.

Mr. Ben shoved his gun out at the door and fired over him. Sim Drogus dived into shadows like a frog into a pond.

"What poor shooting, Mr. Gray," mocked Brooke Altic's voice from somewhere behind his tree. "Or possibly you only meant to scare him. If so, you did that. But keep on shooting, please. When your ammunition is all gone—"

"It ain't all gone yet, God damn your time," Mr. Ben

busted in at the top of his voice. "We got plenty more bullets here, and one of 'em's got your name wrote out on it, loud and clear. Just you step into view, just step."

"A highly intriguing offer, but I must decline with thanks," Altic drawled to us. "However, if you're going to be so inhospitable to Mr. Drogus, here present are some other neighbors who would like to talk to you."

We waited. At last: "Mr. Ben?" questioned a man's voice. "Mr. Ben Gray?"

"Sure as I'm born, that there bank-jumping, side-changing Lew Replogle," grated Mr. Ben, as hoarse as a rasp on rusty iron. "I'll tell him a thing or two he should ought to know about himself."

"No, let me do the talking," I said, and waved at him to hold his words. I put up my own voice. "Mr. Replogle, what is it you want?"

"Is that John I hear a-talking?" said Replogle, and now I could make him out and two others, a-standing together in the road just before the head of the path. "We want to tell Mr. Ben something."

"You can tell it to me, if there's aught to be told," I said. "What do you want?"

"Just only a peaceable message to give," said Replogle. "John, me and you met this day and shook hands to be friends. Here with me I've got Matty Groves and U. G. Bannion, who did likewise. Now, we want to do this thing right, do it peaceable."

"Do it peaceable, you say?" I asked him out yonder. "And if you can't do it peaceable, you reckon to do it the other way?"

"Well—"

He didn't go on, but, a-straining my eyes, I saw that those three men had guns out there to lean on.

"You reckon you'll make a fight here, rush this cabin?" I

said. "Mr. Replogle, you don't seem to be gifted enough to see how the Shonokins are a-fixing to use you. They themselves can't stand gunfire. They're afraid one of them will get himself killed and the rest will have to run off and quit."

"And that's right enough the lowdown Shonokin way," husked Mr. Ben beside me.

"I count three of you there, in the pay of Brooke Altic," I went on, "and if Sim Drogus is still round there with you, that makes four human men who might could face up to some shooting. All right, but there's five of us in here, and we have guns and we can use them right well. Did you air hear tell that tale of how the monkey got the cat to drag the hot chestnuts out of the fire? You can get more than your paw burnt here."

"John, I ain't none used to be talked to thataway," said Replogle, "and I don't like it."

"Nor I don't like to talk along such lines myself," I told him. "But we mean business in here, whatair kind of business comes up. And if I was you, or Mr. Groves, or Mr. Bannion, I'd pull up and leave out of here and hope I had a whole skin."

"Well—" he said again.

I watched them fade away out of sight amongst trees somewhere.

"This is all part of desperation tactics on the part of the Shonokins," said Warren, who still stayed at the table. "Remember, they consider themselves an endangered species, and just now they're acting accordingly."

"I'll endanger their old tore-down species," vowed Mr. Ben. "Give me just air kind of a good chance, and I'll make them so scarce and hard to find, folks will pay good money to look at them in a circus."

Hazel Techeray actually laughed. I near about did myself.

At the table, Warren had twitched open that paper wad, and he was a-studying the alexandrite. A ray of light came from the lamp Hazel Techeray had set down again, and struck to the table. I saw the alexandrite shine red and fiery in it. That thing looked as hot as a coal on the hearth. I wondered if it would blaze up at us.

"They want it," said Warren softly. "They're trying to involve it in something."

The cabin creaked, but not so heavy and tingly now.

"Give it up," the voice of Brooke Altic rang to us. "Give it up. It's no good to Ben Gray except as a souvenir. In our hands, it can benefit the world."

"Benefit men and women?" I called a challenge to him. "Or just only Shonokins?"

"Benefit men and women who help us," said Brooke Altic. "Even you, John."

"You counted me out of it once," I reminded him through a space in the logs.

"You can still square accounts with us, and profit," he said. "Get Ben Gray to give it up. Otherwise, you won't last out the night. We're concentrating attention on you. That's a promise, John, a promise I'll be able to keep."

He talked out yonder in the night. A night thing, that's what you might could call Brooke Altic. I recollected tales about other night things, how they left their graves at sundown and drank the blood of sleeping folks. The Shonokins had ways just that bad, if they could fetch them off.

"I mean every word I say," he told us, and fell quiet. The creaking and rocking of the cabin started in again.

I looked toward the table where Warren had put down the alexandrite. It made a little crumb of fire there, stronger than just the lamplight on it. I braced myself on that rocking floor.

"What's a-happening there?" I inquired Warren.

"I'm not quite sure. All I know is, there's power in this jewel. I wonder—wonder—"

He leaned his rifle to a chair back. "Where's a knife?" he called.

XIV

"Knife?" Callie repeated as she came in from the back room where she'd been on watch.

"A knife, and quick," he said, the sharpest I could imagine him a-talking to her.

"Here," she said, and ran to the sink and fetched back a carving knife. I could see its whetted edge shine out. He took it, and I wondered what he was up to as he turned it over and over.

"It's been blessed already, coming from your hand to me," he said to Callie, "but I must do even more, with what words I remember."

He clutched the knife against him with both hands and ducked his head down. The house creaked as he did that. I reckoned that he said some kind of prayer.

"All right now!" he halfway shouted all of a sudden.

With the point of the knife he shoved the alexandrite to the dead center of the table. "Clear these things off here, Callie," he said, like an order. "I'm going to need all the room there possibly is."

She and Hazel Techeray quick whisked away some bowls and cups and spoons. The house made its rattle all round us, though this time I didn't hear that wind. Warren took the knife and began to gouge a long, straight line in the wood of the table top. He cut another line, and then another, then two more. He made them into the shape of a five-pointed star there, with the alexandrite at the middle of it, a-shining more like a fire coal than ever.

"What in the world are you a-doing?" I wondered him, but he said nair word back. He shifted the knife in his hand and dragged the point strong to dig a circle all round outside the five points of his star.

"I know," chattered Hazel Techeray, a-watching. "I know what that there thing is. Ain't nair seen one before, but I've heard tell of them. I've heard them called—"

"It's called a pentacle," said Warren, a-straightening himself up and a-dropping the knife. "Now, where's that pencil John used with the plate?"

He took it, and the house shook all round us as he wrote big letters inside each point of the star.

"Mr. Warren, you dead certain sure of what you're a-doing?" Hazel Techeray squeaked to him. "Them's the names of the Five Kings of the North!"

"That's right," he said. "A pentacle can defend both the body and the soul, if they deserve to be defended."

Outside, the wind made its howl again, and the thunder gave a roll like a barrel of stones a-running downhill.

"All right now," said Warren. "Come here, everybody. I need you."

"Who's a-going to stay on watch?" asked Mr. Ben.

"I need you," said Warren again. "Here's our pentacle, and the alexandrite is its center of help to us. Somebody must stand at each of the five points. Come here, John. You stand beside me."

I came there. Callie drew up on his other side. In front of me, a word was written in the nearest point of the star. HALANTA, I thought it said. The word in the point toward Warren looked to be ZITRAEL, and in the one toward Callie, THANAOR. Mr. Ben came and stood at a point marked TALOUK. Next to him was Hazel Techeray, and her point had the name ZITRAMI. That's the best I recollect. Just now, I'm not sure in my mind I want to know if those names are spelled right or not. We all kept hold of our guns, all but Hazel Techeray, who hadn't been given one, and Jackson Warren, who'd leaned his away.

"We're all a-going to get ourselves destroyed with this," said Hazel Techeray, a-shaking where she'd stood herself at ZITRAMI.

"We'll hope not," said Warren, a-motioning to make us all stand just at the star points.

"Then names looks heathen to me," said Mr. Ben.

"Heathen or not, I'll call on them. Quiet, now."

He flung up his arms high and spoke:

"You Five Kings," he said, "assist me, who have the boldness to name you, whom no man should name and invoke save when in great danger."

Thunder sort of moaned outside. Lightning flashed its glow in at the log spaces. I thought Hazel Techeray would fall over.

"We are in great peril of soul and body," Warren spaced his words out slow. "Pardon me if I have sinned in any manner, for I trust in your protection."

I stood there where he'd put me to stand. I made no move, said no word. They'd chosen me the captain to defend that cabin, but here I had to give over to Warren. He knew what he was a-doing. Or anyway, I hoped he did.

There came another big, whanging rattle of thunder and lightning.

"They're a-fetching more storm on us," whined Hazel Techeray.

"I think that happens to be our own storm," said Warren, and as he spoke there rose up a wild wail all round the place: The Shonokins, and not a laugh this time. Something pestered them.

"Stop in there, stop, stop!" yelled Brooke Altic to us.

"We've penned up the jewel," said Warren, so softly he was hard to hear talk, even when I stood next to him. "They were focused on it. Now they know they can't reach it."

Thunder, thunder, and lightning, lightning.

"You can't do that!" Brooke Altic was a-yammering.

Nothing back from Warren, nair reply to Brooke Altic. Warren lifted his two hands again and spoke more slow-spaced words:

"Preserve us from evil spirits," he halfway sang. "Help us to bind and destroy the evil spirits, and reconcile the good ones to us. Be our sins forgiven, be they washed whiter than snow."

I looked at the name in my star point. HALANTA. I wondered myself who Halanta was. I wondered who those others were, called by Hazel Techeray the Five Kings of the North. I asked in my soul about what a pentacle might could do, where it came from, who first knew the way to draw one. I got no answer. But the tempest storm made its voice heard over our cabin roof. And, midmost of the star, that alexandrite stared like a shining red eye at me. I had the notion that smoke began to curl around it.

I cut a look at Jackson Warren. His face was tenched up like as if it had been pulled tight all round and pegged down at the edges like a banjo head. His skin shown white and gleamy. I thought his hair stood up stiff as a brush. He was all the way into what he was a-trying to do.

"I call, I call," he was a-saying. "I call, you Five Kings, and judge if I and my cause are worthy. I commit unto you these enemies; I call on you to judge them truly."

I felt that if I looked round, there'd be something close behind me. Something I'd be purely scared to see. But I didn't look round. I set my eyes back on the flame-shining alexandrite.

Outside, the wailing cry again, all round and round the house. It sounded like pain, bad pain.

"They're in trouble, I vow," growled out Mr. Ben, beside his TALOUK point of the star.

"Yes," said Warren, tight as a fiddle string. "Yes, because it's our storm now, not theirs. The Five Kings answer us."

They answered us, sure enough, right then. You should ought to have heard the drum roll of that thunder.

Warren hiked his hands higher toward the rafters over him, and he turned his face up, too.

"Five," he rolled out. "You are five, and the points of the pentacle are five, and the number five has great force in holy things. There are the five fingers on a hand, the five toes on a foot. There are the five senses—tasting, smelling, hearing, seeing, touching. Five is a number that will send away bad spirits, expel deadly poisons." He drew his breath in, hard. "It is a number full of majesty, a vehicle of human life."

"Human life," I echoed him to myself, while I recollected that the Shonokins took their pride in being something other than human.

I looked back at the alexandrite. It burned, sure enough. It scorched its place into the wood of the table top, made the wood black.

"You can't!" screamed a voice at us from outside, and this time I nair thought it was Brooke Altic.

"We can," said Warren, loud and clear as a man a-making a speech. "We can do what we do. We do it against the force and will of evil."

It was near about like a wink of the eye that alexandrite made. A darkening and a brightening, hot and trembly. I had the feeling of a grip on me, not like that tingly grip out on the Shonokin track. I told myself to be glad of that grip. It was from something on my side, the human side of things.

Outside, there beat up voices. "No! No!" A whole bunch of them a-saying that, and up over them all, Brooke Altic: "You seal your doom, you seal your doom—"

But in the room with us, a whispery sound in the air, friendly.

"You are welcome here, you noble Five Kings," rang out Warren. "We have called you here by the great name to which every knee is bowed, in this world and in the next."

He pointed his finger to the alexandrite. It sort of puffed and smoked there, and the light in it died down, and it laid like a cinder.

There came a scratching on the logs of the cabin outside, all the way round, front and back, like hands a-picking at the walls. The wailing voices made their sad, awful sound out yonder. Brooke Altic's voice screamed:

"What are you trying to do? What are you going to do?"

Not one of us replied him that, but we knew that something was a-being done. The jewel he'd wanted from us, the jewel he would have tied his power to, would have used to rule us, was no jewel now. It crumbled where it lay on the scorched table, like an ash dropped off a cigar. I saw a black burnt place on the wood.

A whole beating storm of hands then, loud as the hail had been.

"Let's stand them off," said Mr. Ben under his breath.

"Stay where you are," Warren bade him, and raised his voice again.

"In triumph we finish here," he said. "In triumph we finish here. The teeth of the snake are drawn."

The heavy press of air fell off round us. It was like as if people had been there in the room with us, and had gone. But just then the front door swung itself open, and there stood Brooke Altic.

He wore the fancy clothes he'd worn last time I'd seen him. But they were mussed up, muddy, like as if he'd been a-crawling round like a snake. His shirt collar was all torn open at his throat, and his hair, so combed out before, strung thisaway and that round his face. His eyes stuck out at us, his mouth was open, and his sharp teeth gnashed themselves at us.

"You'll pay for all this," he gurgled out. "I'll say just one word, one strong word—"

Hazel Techeray had swung off from the table, had left her point of the star. She grabbed up the rifle Warren had leaned to the chair. She shoved it almost into Altic's wide eye and pulled trigger.

Bang!

I saw the blood jump out all over his white face in the lamplight. And over he slammed down on his back, like as if he'd been snatched there by a rope, right down he went across the threshold of the open door.

Outside then, there sounded a cry fit to pop your ears. It must have been all the Shonokins a-yelling at once.

That same moment, the churning sound of feet on the dead run, on the run out of the yard, on the run away from where Brooke Altic had been killed dead.

XV

And after the running, no sound. You heard the silence.

I can't say for certain today what hour of the night Brooke Altic was shot down and his people run off to leave him there. All I do know is that the five of us waited in that cabin, the five of us with him flung out where he'd fallen across the sill of the door and the door open so he was half in and half out. We waited there till the stars paled out with the early, early dawn.

And, gentlemen, it was a devil of a long time to wait. We didn't do much talking, I recollect. I felt some surprised at Hazel Techeray, who, from when first she came in the house, had trembled and shaken and shed tears. Now she was the steadiest of us all, the way I look back on it. One thing she did was to heat up what coffee we had left in the pot. It had gone as cold as well water, and the second heating made it stout and bitter. But I was right glad to take a cupful and work at it.

As for Mr. Ben, after while he picked up that rifle Hazel Techeray had used on Brooke Altic and carried it to a chair with his gun-cleaning gear. He worked the bolt lever to shake the shells out of it, and put them in a little heap on another chair. Then he cleaned the gun, and not in my life have I seen as many guns cleaned so clean. Finally he loaded it up again and snapped the safety catch on and took it to his cupboard and racked it up there.

Warren and Callie sat together next to the hearth where

no fire burned, and they talked about what I reckon was their own business and nobody else's.

But, the way I say, dawn was a-coming at last. Mr. Ben finished the coffee he was a-drinking and got up on his feet.

"John," he said, "and you, Jackson, come along, give me a hand with what's got to be done."

We knew what he meant. The three of us went to where Brooke Altic lay through the door, and stooped down to pick him up. His eyes stared up at us, dull and empty, with the pupil like just an up-and-down slit. His body was as limp as a wet sock, not stiffed out like a man's body. We wagged him down off the porch, and out along the path to where that track was.

"Here," said Mr. Ben, and we laid him down, and Mr. Ben went to his shed and fetched back a couple of spades and a grubbing hoe.

We got at our work and digging. All of us had strong arms and backs. We hollowed out that grave—six feet long and two feet wide and nearabout four deep—in about an hour in the early sun. Nair one of us said a word while we dug. We didn't even look in one another's faces. Finally we picked Altic up again and laid him in the hole. He was so small he didn't crowd it.

I pulled his hands across his chest. His beautiful ring shone on one. They felt cold, with the third finger the longest and those claws on them for nails, as I laid them one on top of the other. Mr. Ben fished out a red handkerchief from his pants pocket and spread it on the fishy-pale face. We stood up round the grave.

"One of youins want to say a word for him?" Mr. Ben asked. "Might could you do it, John?"

I wondered what could be said. I recollected something of the old burial service I'd heard again and again, and tried with that:

"In the midst of life, we are in death. Ashes to ashes, dust to dust."

No more than that. I thought some about a prayer, but what prayer of mine would Brooke Altic welcome to be said for him?

We picked up the spades and covered him in. We patted the dirt down solid all over the top.

"That'll grow up with grass right away," allowed Mr. Ben. "And he guarantees us that no more Shonokins will come a-using round from this on."

He carried the tools back to their shed. When we came to the porch again, Hazel Techeray was a-scrubbing out some blood stains with handfuls of gritty soil. We all went in and washed up. I don't think we felt hungry, but we had more of that hot, stout coffee and some cold corn bread and butter.

"I'm a-going to go to the Shonokin settlement," I said then.

"Me, I'll come with you," said Mr. Ben. "And I'll take me along a gun, and you'd best do the same."

"This time I sure will," I agreed him.

Out on the way, I felt no jangle, no hum in me. That Shonokin power had gone from their track. The thing they'd started to do, it was all finished. All that spell of Warren's, and the death of Altic, it had plumb silenced and ended their work.

We passed along to where the balanced rock was. It was balanced no more. The top piece was fallen off from where it had teetered. I walked up to it and all round. Its power was gone off. Gone to what place it had come from, and I couldn't guess that place.

At last the settlement. But different now.

It was tumbledown. That gardinel at its edge looked all fallen in, like a rotten pumpkin in a field. The roofs of the shelters sagged, the windows were as blank as the eyes of dead Brooke Altic. In those circle-shaped lots, the finger-bushes and other plants looked all limped over and withered away.

"I swear," said Mr. Ben, a-leaning on his gun, "this here place looks to have been left out of, fifty years ago."

It was true. It was deserted. The Shonokins were gone, after their power was driven out of them. Where? Some other place was all I could say. Wherever it was, whatever they'd do now, it wouldn't be round here.

Mr. Ben turned heavy on his heel and we started back down the way that had lost its jangle and buzz forever. I recollect how I looked at the trees that yesterday had seemed to bunch up and stare at me. Now they were just common trees. I heard a grasshopper make its chirp. It sounded as pretty to me as the sweetest song of air bird I could call for.

Still we didn't talk much. It was better than halfway back that we saw two folks a-coming along toward us—little Callie and Jackson Warren, a-walking hand in hand. We came up to them, and I told them how the Shonokins had left out of their settlement.

"Where's Miss Hazel?" Mr. Ben wanted to know.

"She went back home," said Callie. "She said, her kind regards."

"Hmmm," said Mr. Ben. "Maybe I'll go over there some time, go over and see her. Be neighbors to her."

"Callie and I have something to tell you," said Warren. He smiled, the first smile air one of us had tried on for who could say how long. "Mr. Ben, I want to marry Callie."

"Hmmm," droned Mr. Ben again. "I can't rightly say you surprise me none. I'd be a gone gump if I hadn't seen that thing a-coming. But what I want to hear tell is, what does Callie want?"

3

"Daddy," she said, a-hanging tight to Warren's hand, "I say I want to marry Jackson."

All four of us walked back together toward the cabin.

"Well, it ain't for me to say no," said Mr. Ben. "Callie's wish is always my wish."

"And, John," said Warren to me, "will you stand up with us at the wedding?"

"I'd be proud to, Jackson," I said.

All the trouble and danger seemed to flow off from us like so much running water.